The Chief Complaint

Element VFD #1

MJ Buck

ISBN: 0-9824696-8
ISBN-13: 978-0-9824696-0-6

DEDICATION

For my parents, who believed in my potential even when I didn't and to my husband, for being my best friend and my hero.

ONE

James Whitmore. The Deputy Chief of the Element Volunteer Fire Department stood with his arms folded and locked across his chest, glowering at the growing crowd of people in the station activities hall.

"Damn it Gus, it's the same thing every year."

He glanced sideways, and down, at the portly middle-aged figure next to him as he spoke.

Gus Barnes had been the Chief of the Volunteer Fire Department for years and likely would be again after tonight's annual election of officers. In a town of less than 3,000 people there is a very limited number of people who are qualified to be the Fire Chief. To be precise, there were exactly two, Gus and James.

Gus glanced up at his companion, surveying the silver blonde hair and green eyes atop the square-jawed face and six foot four inch frame. By comparison Gus was only average height, overweight (he preferred to think of it as under-tall), with mousy brown hair. What was left of his hair at any rate. Standing next to the younger man's Viking figure always left Gus feeling a bit inadequate somehow.

James continued to scowl as he examined the crowd gathering in the room.

"I don't' know why you bother to send a van over to

Middleton Retirement Home to pick up all these old fossils anyway."

Gus smiled fondly as his gaze homed in on the half dozen elderly men, mostly in wheelchairs. They were all in theirs eighties and nineties and had been charter members when the fire station was first established a half century ago. If asked, most of them would happily spend hours telling hair raising tales about having to hitch horses up to wagons in order to get the pumps and hoses to a fire scene.

"They are life members of the station and therefore entitled to cast their votes. Just like any other member."

"Yeah, I guess so." James' face clearly showed his doubts. "But it isn't as if you need their votes. Everyone knows that the two of us are the only ones eligible to be the Chief and Deputy Chief."

"That's why you keep losing the top slot to me." Gus smirked. "You just don't understand people."

He nodded in the direction of the senior's contingent as he continued.

"They are life members and that is important to them. This is just about their only chance to feel like they can still contribute something to the department. I make sure that they get this chance to get out and contribute…they vote to keep me on as Chief."

James gave a snort of derision. "Humph! You arrange everyone as if they were pieces on a Chessboard.

"Of course…but the game is called politics, not chess."

He reached up and thumped the younger man between the shoulder blades. The blow landed somewhat more firly that might have been strictly necessary and James stumbled forward a half step before regaining his balance.

"Well, maybe so, but sometime the Good Ole Boys network can be downright irritating."

"That attitude is why you will always be the Deputy Chief…at least as long as I'm around."

Gus went back to watching some of the younger members setting up rows of folding chairs as the crowd continued to filter into the hall. After a few minutes of companionable silence he used an elbow to jab James in the right kidney. When he was sure he had the younger man's attention, he nodded across the room at a group of men in their early and mid-twenties.

"What do you suppose they are up to?"

James glanced over at the group and sighed. "Since Randy Simms seems to be doing all the talking I am willing to bet that they are planning yet another attempt to have the station by-laws changed so they can be eligible to become officers.

Gus bobbed his head up and down in agreement. "Still think we don't need the life members on hand? Not even to squash this little rebellion?"

James sighed again but nodded his acceptance of the logic. It took a two-thirds majority of the entire membership to revise the by-laws and the life members votes would ensure that the change didn't happen. The young hot heads in the department would just have to wait until they were older, and hopefully more mature, before gaining any real authority over anything.

A glance up at the clock showed the time as two minutes to seven pm. James looked down at his companion and smiled.

"Shall we proceed to battle?"

"Oh, by all means," came Gus's reply. "Let the games begin."

###

Half an hour later the debate and mud-slinging portion of the election was in full force. Gus and I had started out with our usual rhetoric but for some reason this year the fun and friendly debate had turned spiteful and we were both caught up in tearing each other down for the crowd. It was something that had never happened before…not even 3 years back when I had an affair with Gus' wife while he was traveling for his job.

"Some of these kids have seen too many Hollywood movies about firefighters and think it's okay to charge on into a burning building without a hose or backup".

Gus looked at me, "At least I don't have them standing around outside, while somebody may be trapped inside the building".

"Damn it Gus, you know as well as I do that rookies are supposed to stay outside the fire until they complete their initial training. I don't want to have to tell the mother of some nineteen year old that he died in a fire when he should never have been inside the building in the first place."

"So, if I arrive on the scene first and only have a rookie with me I should just stand around outside and wait for you to get there, even if there might be somebody trapped inside? I thought that you believed the victim comes first?"

I sighed, "I do, and you know it. However, it doesn't do anybody any good for the rescuer to become a victim either. A dead or injured firefighter isn't going to save anybody."

It was an old argument between us. I think that he tends allow the younger kids to hot dog at the fires and that it is going to get somebody killed someday. In return, he thinks I tend to be too cautious at fires and that it will cost a victim their life one day. I know he believes it's true but what can I say, the NFPA publishes the rules and regulations for firefighters that are designed to try to save lives. I happen to be one of those people who believe that the rules exist for a darn good reason and we should be following them.

The sniping usually continues along this vein, with charges and counter charges about the best way to fight fires and to manage emergency incidents, until the votes are counted.

As the ambient noise began to drop off a voice, pitched to a stage whisper, reached me from someplace off to my left.

"Well, at least he doesn't have to pay alimony anymore."

It seemed oddly out of context when everyone else was so intent on discussing the virtues and vices of the nominees so I turned slightly to discover the source. Randy Simms was holding court nearby. A half dozen of the younger members encircled him, wide-eyed, their jaws slack in mesmerized horror. Knowing full well the kind of nasty rumors that Randy liked to spread, I listened a bit closer, surreptitiously nudging Gus in the ribs to get his attention.

"We all know that the official report said he followed protocol but if you ask me, I think that it was pretty lucky for him that he was the officer in charge of the accident scene. Of course, it didn't turn out so good for Sara."

What the hell was he talking about? This wasn't just his usual gossip; it was an outright accusation. They all turned to look at me as he spoke, their eyes wide with uncertainty. He grinned maliciously.

Five Months earlier:

The accident had been horrific. Five cars lay in mangled heaps, scattered across the highway like so much litter flung onto the pavement by passerby. We had been third ambulance arriving on the scene but only by a matter of moments. As the senior EMT officer present, I had taken control of determining priorities and telling the dispatcher that we needed a MEDEVAC helicopter.

Jill Monroe, the first EMT to have arrived, gave me a quick summary of the situation. Three patients were trapped in their vehicles and would have to be cut free, one of those a man with a severe head injury from apparently hitting the back of the driver's seat face first. The other two did not appear to be seriously injured, just trapped although one woman clearly had a broken arm and both had a variety of minor lacerations. Two other victims were clearly dead, apparently having been killed on impact. In addition, there were several "walking wounded" already out of their vehicles and low on the priorities list.

I radioed back to dispatch asking for an additional paramedic unit, a helicopter for the head injury patient, a rescue squad and a variety of engines and ambulances to cut those trapped from their cars and treat the less severely injured. That done, I turned to doing a more detailed assessment of the patients and giving the crews their assignments.

I was checking on the status of each patient when I stuck my head into the last car and came face to face with Sara; my ex-wife.

Sara and I were divorced but we had parted friends. She couldn't handle the stress of being a firefighter's wife and I couldn't give it up. I didn't blame her. Firefighters sometimes get hurt, and sometimes they get killed. Even if they do survive, burns can be pretty awful to live through. Every time I went on a call, she was terrified that I was going to get hurt or killed. It does happen. I certainly understood her fear, but I just couldn't give it up. Every time the pager went off, I knew that if I didn't show up, perhaps others wouldn't show up, and perhaps somebody would die. I couldn't live with myself knowing that somebody died because nobody showed up to save them.

That's one of the things about being a volunteer fire fighter, you can turn off the pager and go back to sleep, but how do you sleep later on if somebody dies? Sara lived in fear of me getting hurt and I lived in fear of not being at the scene on a call when one more person might have made the difference. She looked up at me from inside the mangled car and smiled.

"I knew you had to be around here somewhere".

She looked pale and wane but otherwise in surprisingly good shape considering the state of the car wrapped around her. She was only visible from about the waist up; everything below that was hidden by the dashboard and steering wheel that were pressed against her, pinning her in place.

"Oh my God Sara, are you OK?"

It was probably the most inane thing I have ever said to an accident victim but she took it in stride.

"Sure. I just can't move anything below my waist. Trapped…y'know?"

She waved her left hand matter-of-factly at the dashboard holding her down.

"Bet I'm gonna have some hellacious bruises later on. But right now, I'm just glad that you didn't quit the department when I wanted you to. I feel a lot better knowing that you are here to make sure things get done right."

One of the EMT's recited her vital signs to me and commented that her only apparent injury was a broken right arm that had already been splinted and that a cervical collar had been put on her neck as a precaution. Considering the condition of the car (the entire front end was compressed to about half normal size and most of that was pushed into the front seat) it was amazing that she was alive much less in such good shape. That was also why I had directed that the other two patients be extricated first; head trauma and a flail chest (caused when the steering wheel breaks every rib, crushing the breastbone against the heart) have medical priority over broken arms. Even if I had known that Sara was in the third car, the injuries dictated the order of care.

I stayed with her as the crew of the rescue squad used the Hearst tool (commonly called the Jaws of Life) to cut open the twisted metal that surrounded her; my hand holding hers through the open window, both of us buried under a turnout coat for protection from flying shards of glass and metal from the cutting tools.

When the scream of protesting metal finally stopped and they lifted away the coat we both blinked in the sudden glare of the afternoon sun. As I let go of her hand to step out of the way, so they could finally lift the dash she smiled at me.

"I never stopped loving you."

The mass of metal and plastic pulled away and Jill moved in to check for any additional injuries that might have been hidden below it. A moment later Jill's frantic cry brought me back to the car.

Sara's head lolled to one side, her face deathly white. A gurgling rattle escaped her lips once, and then there was silence.

Heedless of what other injuries she might have, I dragged her out of the vehicle and onto the waiting backboard while frantically trying to get CPR started and yelling for help. Moments later Jill grabbed my arm.

"She's gone," a voice said in my ear, "look at her."

I shook her off, continuing my frenzied efforts. It took three of them to finally make me stop and really look at her. A massive wound ran across her midsection, almost completely cutting her in half. They pointed to the remains of the dashboard, a large flat blade of metal; stained crimson was now visible, sticking out from the underside. Jill shook me again.

"It must have been driven in during the accident. There was no way to see it until we moved the dash and then it was too late. Moving the dash pulled it out and she was gone in seconds."

Ignoring everyone and everything else around me I turned back to Sara. I knelt down next to her, holding her icy hand. I was still there when the coroner arrived to collect her and the others that had not survived.

The autopsy determined that the metal had acted like a blade, slicing her in half from front to back, stopping only when it embedded itself in her spine. Damage to the spinal cord higher up had prevented her from feeling any pain from the injury and the weight of the dashboard pressed against her had held the metal in place, sealing the wound. Like a water tight door on a ship holding back the sea, the seal had prevented her from bleeding to death when the accident happened. When the removal of the dash had released the pressure and revealed the injury, she bled out within moments.

I was pretty broken up for a while after Sara's death; didn't want to get in the ambulance at all for a long time. It's the kind of thing that is bound to happen if you do this long enough; a patient goes bad and there is no way to predict it or stop it; or a fire goes bad and somebody gets hurt, because you didn't know about the 5 gallon gasoline container some idiot had stored in a back closet. It's a lot harder when it's somebody you know, somebody you care about. Eventually a call came in while I was at the station and there wasn't anybody else to ride the Officer's right seat, so I went. After that, it got a little easier. Even so, I still don't like riding the gut wagon very much these days.

"I certainly wouldn't want him working on me if I were in an accident."

I don't even know the words to describe how I felt. Gut punched, seeing red, blazing mad...none of them seem to cover it very well. Let's just say that I lost my cool at that point and things escalated out of control pretty fast. I looked at Gus to see if he would shut them down but his expression was blank. It may have been shock, but at the time, I thought he was agreeing with them so I retaliated.

"At least I don't keep a bottle of Jack Daniels in my desk drawer here at the station."

I didn't mention that the unopened bottle was covered with a thick layer of dust and had been there for years, having been left by his predecessor.

Now Gus was just as ticked off as I was.

"At least I'm not sleeping with my best friend's wife."

I wasn't either, at least not anymore. My short lived affair with his wife, three years ago just after my divorce, had been over almost as quickly as it begun once he found out about it.

"No, you just invite young female firefighters and EMTs for 'special' one-on-one training when the station is empty."

Janice, a young rookie, had been locking up on the scene because she was afraid of making mistakes. Gus had been working with her, trying to bolster her confidence in her own skills. I let the statement hang out there in front of the crowd without explanation, leading people to believe that he had been getting a little action on the side. After his comment about my affair with Carla, it made him out to be a major hypocrite.

Anyway, you get the picture, conspiracy theorists on the left, moral high ground on the right, everyone else trapped in between. Both Gus and I were red-faced and shouting, right along with a lot of other folks by the time the president finally began to bang his gavel and call for order to proceed with the formal election. I didn't even bother to stick around for the actual voting.

"You like the power don't you?" I hollered at Gus. "I've had it with you playing games with our lives. You won't ever give it up. You'll continue to lord it over the rest of us until the day you die."

I grabbed my gear and stomped out of the station, heading for home.

Three hours later Gus was found dead in the bunk room at the back of the station.

Billy Henderson, a young member who was living in the station after breaking up with his girlfriend recently, had gone to the bunk room to get some sleep and found Gus slumped over on one of the bunks, his insulin kit opened nearby, not breathing, no pulse. Billy shouted for help and began CPR. They worked on him as hard as they could, but by the time they got to the ER, it was obvious that he was gone. Everyone in the station knew that with Gus gone, the Chief's hat came to me. They had also been witness to the fury we had both been dishing out. That is how I ended up being arrested for murder right in front of everyone, less than a week later. Being home alone getting drunk wasn't much of an alibi.

TWO

Wednesday afternoon the members of the station, along with most of the rest of the residents of the town, gathered at the Willets funeral home, which was tucked just out of sight, one block off Main Street near the east end of town. The parking lot had overflowed early and cars were parked across the street in the Piggly Wiggly parking lot. Out front of the funeral home, the engine and the wagon were parked with their lights running to guide the members in. Both vehicles were draped with black crepe bunting along the sides. The bunting has long been the traditional sign of mourning for fire stations. Similar black crepe had been draped across the front of the station in huge graceful curves, just above the bay doors and hanging down along the sides of the left and right doors.

Before the first of the mourners arrived, the casket had been moved into place at the far end of the viewing room. The dark wood blending in with the equally dark paneling of the room so that the cream colored velvet lining on which Gus was resting stood out brilliantly from its position centered against the wall. Thick carpeting muted the sound of footsteps and seemed to absorb the voices of those present and contributing to the hushed feeling of that somber space. Earlier that afternoon and from the moment it had been placed in its position of honor there had been two firefighters standing post in honor of the Chief. In full dress uniform with black bands across the face of their silver firefighters badges to indicate that they were in mourning the members stood, one at the head and one of the foot of the casket.

Every 10 minutes they would rotate out and two new members would take their place in a formal routine that had been carefully practiced until it was done with military precision, the turns made in sharp pivoting motions as if their feet were rotating on the head of a pin. The rotation of those standing guard over the casket would continue throughout the afternoon and evening as mourners came and went paying their respects to a man they had known all of their lives.

Element isn't big enough to support a fire department Honor Guard but being close to the county corner, three County Fire Associations had formed a tri-county guard that performed this function with depressing regularity.

Lights tucked discreetly behind the flower arrangements and up into the bulkheads around the ceiling cast a soft, luminous glow across the room supplementing the many candles that burned in tall gleaming brass holders. Mourners came and went, the tide ebbing and flowing like the ocean, the murmur of hushed voices providing a counterpoint to the strains of Mozart's Requiem that emanated from unseen speakers like the voice of a ghostly choir.

Around the sides of the room, tables had been set up, draped in white linen, displaying pictures and items that had been important to him during his life. The tables alternated with flower arrangements so that there was no place that you could stand to look at the pieces of his story without the scent of flowers providing a backdrop to your thoughts. On one table rested his white Chief's helmet, bearing the stains of soot from fires throughout the years. Nearby was the ornate brass fire horn that had been presented to him when he was first installed as Chief. There were pictures of him as a cadet in his teens and again as a rookie when he attended the Fire Academy upstate. His turnout gear, smelling faintly of smoke even over the scent of carnations and lilies, hung on a rack in a corner of the room near the foot of the casket.

Throughout the afternoon Gus' wife Carla stood near the door, shaking hands and accepting condolences from the seemingly endless stream of people. She looked so gray and worn that I wondered how she was holding up inside. Carla is a strong woman, but I know that her entire life had been centered on her marriage to Gus for a long time. It sometimes seemed that her entire goal in life had been to live up to the appellation of, "a good wife" and she had seemed entirely content in that role. As far as I knew the only time that she had broken free of the mold had been three years ago when Gus was traveling for work and she had been kind of adrift without him to take care of. Something of an introvert, she really hadn't known what to do with herself and the empty hours while Gus was gone, nor had she had many close friends of her own. At the same time, I had just gone through my divorce from Sara and was just as much adrift. Like leaves floating down the river, we had been caught in the same current and it had carried us together for a little while in a less torrid than companionable affair. It had ended as soon as Gus had returned home and stopped traveling.

In the end, when the last of the mourners had left for the evening, Carla was pale and limp with exhaustion. She walked slowly over to look down at Gus lying peacefully against the cream velvet lining of the casket . He was wearing his dress firefighter's uniform, with the jacket split up the back so that it appeared to fit well instead of the buttons pulling across the chest the way it normally did. With the heavy makeup that had been applied by the mortician in an attempt to give his face a healthy glow; he looked more like a plastic mannequin than the man who'd been vital and active until two days earlier. The two firefighters standing by the casket stared straight ahead as if trying to avoid being witnesses to her pain. For a long time she stood and stared down at the man who had been the center of her life. I wondered what she was thinking and feeling at that moment. After several long silent minutes she seemed to simply fold up like a paper doll, sinking gracefully down to her knees before tilting over to lean sideways against the casket, crying.

Up to that point, I had been respecting her privacy and allowing her to grieve. Nevertheless, I really couldn't stand by any longer and allow her to go through it alone. I walked up the length of the room to join her, noticing as I did that the music had stopped. The silence seemed to accentuate that the music had gone out of her life as well. Stooping down next to her, I put out a hand and called her name softly; the next thing I knew she was in my arms, crying hysterically. I just sat there and held her, at a complete loss for words. I'm not sure how long we stayed like that, but eventually as the tears began to subside, I looked up at the stoic faces of the two firefighters standing guard over the scene and asked them to help me get her up from the floor. It basically took all three of us to move her from her place at her husband's side to a nearby chair. If we had been living in a society that used funeral pyres instead of caskets and burial plots; I could easily have believed her capable of throwing herself onto the pyre with him at that point.

I sat next to her for very long time holding her hand and telling her that I too had loved Gus. That he had been like a brother to me. I kept repeating all the platitudes that she had heard from the endless stream of people. While they were true, somehow I felt like it was cheating to say them. There should have been more; more soothing, more emotional, more caring, more 'something', that I could've said to be helpful at that moment. Eventually, someone called Carla's sister to come and get her. None of us felt like she should be alone that night and it certainly wouldn't have been appropriate for her to stay with me. Although if she had asked me, I certainly would have allowed her to. That's what friends are for.

The next morning at Gus' burial, the weather was cold and cloudy with a clammy drizzle that made everything seem that much drearier; as if the heavens were trying to accurately reflect our mood. At 10 o'clock, the casket had been moved from the funeral home and placed in front of the altar at the Baptist church Gus had attended most of his life. The rich color of the solid mahogany casket created a patch of darkness against the luminous marble of the raised dais, framed by the rich cream brocade of the altar cloth behind it. On the closed lid, a gilt Maltese cross glimmered in the filtered light of stained-glass windows, shining like a flame against the dark wood as if proclaiming to the world that here lay a true firefighter.

Once again, the honor guards took their silent places at

head and foot of the coffin. Unlike the night before this time, the sound of their footsteps was almost deafening on the marble floor as they march up to the casket. The precision in which the movements were carried out had been instilled in the members of the honor guard by Gus after he had returned from a tour in the Marine Corps. He had been the one who taught them this maneuver and they performed it flawlessly now, in his honor. After one last check of uniforms and equipment, the silence was broken by the click of the heavy metal plates on the heels of their shoes coming together. When the first loud click was heard, they formed up the first team on the line standing side by side at parade rest, feet slightly apart, hands clasped at the small of their backs. The sound was almost deafening in the quiet room as they marched up to the casket and rendered crisp salutes. Click! Right face and move two steps to side to be at the head and foot of the casket. Click! Turn to face the family and fellow firefighters. The guard leader did an about face and moved back down the aisle. At his third step, the posts moved back to stand at parade rest.

Reading the eulogy had been incredibly hard because I had known Gus most of my life. He had been my mentor as a rookie and my inspiration for many years as Chief. Regardless of the recent events, he had been my friend for far longer than he had been my opponent. I was going to miss him almost as much as I had missed Sara…almost. It felt a bit like losing a parent or a brother rather than just a guy you worked with. Gus had been at the station for thirty six years, starting out as a cadet during high school. Nobody had worked harder or cared more about this town and these people than he had during those years. I felt incredibly guilty over the way that last argument had played out, angry words that I would never be able to take back. Now he was gone and everyone was wondering what would happen next.

After the service at the church, the casket was loaded into the hose bed of the classic nineteen thirty six engine that was the station's pride and joy. The engine had been polished by the station cadets until it seemed to glow with a light of its own from within. The hose had been removed from the bed on the back to make room for the casket and black crepe bunting had been draped along the side rails of the hose bed. Had there been any hint of Sun that day the reflection of the highly polished red paint along the sides of the wagon, combined with the gleaming chrome would have been blinding. It was just under a mile from the church to the cemetery so we walked behind the engine the entire way. Carla walked behind the engine. As acting Chief, I walked beside her so that she didn't have to do it alone. With the rest of the members of the station behind us in uniformed ranks, followed by a couple of guys from Miller's Crossing that played the bagpipes and came over to make sure that Gus had a proper sendoff. We had asked the department in the neighboring town of Edgewood to cover our station for the rest of the day so that the entire station could turn out for the funeral. Most of the guys would end up down at Hank's Place later on, because it had been Gus' favorite after hours hangout, when he wasn't on call at the station. For now, we just walked silently through the drizzle, the bagpipes wailing in the background.

At the gates to the cemetery were two ladder trucks, one from our town, and one which had been borrowed from a nearby community. They had been parked on either side of the entrance way so that the ladders were fully extended and crossed high above the center of the roadway, like crossed swords in a military arch. The crews of both trucks stood beside their vehicles, rigidly at attention they saluted the engine carrying Gus passing between them.

Bagpipes have to be the perfect instrument for a funeral, which was probably why they were traditional for firefighter and cop funerals. As soon as the first rasping notes drift out, tears begin to well up and knees get weak. Mixed with black draped trucks and ranks of men in uniforms marching slowly to the strains of Amazing Grace; nobody can stay in control very well. I certainly was no exception. Of course, I had to stay strong in front of everybody else. I had to be there for Carla, and provide an example of strong leadership to keep the department from falling apart. Losing someone who had been around for as many years as Gus was bound to leave people feeling a bit adrift and without somebody at the helm providing a strong example, it's easy for a volunteer organization to simply disintegrate. I walked straight and solemn but dry eyed to his grave, Carla's hand hooked through my arm so that she could lean on me for support.

Firefighter funerals were kind of like military funerals, there were so many traditions that it's almost like acting out a script. I was glad of that because it made it easier to get through. As I handed Carla the folded flag, speaking words of condolence that were mostly a formality, I remembered the look on her face when she saw me pull up to the curb in front of their house in the Chief's buggy, walking up to the door with the station chaplain beside me. She had already known what we were going to say before she opened the door. Every firefighter's wife knows this scene, lives in fear of it. This was what had driven Sara away from me three years ago, the fear of seeing that damned red car pull up with the chaplain in it. The look on Carla's face made me understand Sara's terror like nothing else ever had. She had been dry eyed but she seemed to age ten years between opening the door and sitting on the sofa. A folded flag just seemed so inadequate at this point, so did the time-honored words.

We had enjoyed our brief affair years earlier and managed to stay cordial when it ended, so it wasn't really surprising that she was holding on to me as we walked to the grave. She really didn't have anybody else; Gus had been her whole life in recent years.

As they folded the flag draping the coffin and passed it to me to present to Carla, I wondered who had killed him. Ever since the police had come by the station the day before and told us that it looked like Gus' death might have been murder, I had been racking my brain trying to figure out who would have hated him enough to do such a thing. I had been pretty angry with him, but not angry enough to hurt him. I'm more likely to walk away than pick a fight if an argument gets that heated.

A deep bell rang out slowly as the casket was lowered into the grave and for a moment I had felt like I was trapped in something written by Edgar Allen Poe, almost expecting a raven to land on the headstone and scold us for failing to take proper care of one of our own.

As Carla placed a single red rose down onto the top of the casket, the macabre sensation passed, although I couldn't help feeling a little bit like something even more dreadful was about to happen. Firmly pushing the feeling away, I helped her to her feet and we lead the crowd of mourners back to their vehicles. I should have paid more attention to that feeling.

CORONER'S PRELIMINARY REPORT

Decedent is a 52 year old Caucasian male, 5'10", approximately 230 pounds, with dark brown hair and brown eyes. Identifying marks include scar approximately 3x5 inches on the left wrist that appears to be from a burn and a tattoo of a Maltese cross on the left bicep. Death occurred at approximately 11:45 PM on 28 July 2007 based on liver temperature. There are no overt signs of trauma. The body was found on a cot in the Element Volunteer Fire Station, apparently having fallen over from a sitting position. Next to the body was a diabetic insulin kit containing an empty vial and nearby were two syringes, apparently used. Decedent was known to be an insulin dependent diabetic. Blood was drawn and sent to the lab for chemical and toxicological analysis. A sample of the vial contents were also sent to the lab. Blood chemistry shows no drugs or other toxins and blood glucose of 586 mg/dl. The chemical analysis of the vial contents identified a concentrated solution of dextrose and saline. Post Mortem shows no signs of acute disease or internal injury. Some arteriosclerosis is present but not sufficient to be the primary cause of death. Preliminary cause of death is cardiac arrest secondary to diabetic coma probably induced by injection of dextrose instead of insulin.

THREE

Detective Sam Gunne, accompanied by two uniformed deputies, arrived at the fire station about a half hour after everyone had returned from the burial. The ladies auxiliary had cooked a meal, and folks who had been milling about sharing their memories of the Chief were just preparing to sit down at the rows of folding tables that had been set up earlier in the day. They walked in the door of the station and cut through the bay into the large hall looking for their quarry. He was a tall blond man with a drink in his hand, standing in a small group near the bar. All of them were still in their dress uniforms from the funeral. Not being one to display a lot of discretion or finesse, Sam simply walked up to the group and announced,

"James Whitmore, you are under arrest for the murder of Gus Barnes."

Reading from a small white card in his hand to make sure that he didn't forget anything he continued,

"You have the right to remain silent. Anything you say can, and will, be used against you in a court of law. You have the right to have an attorney present during questioning. If you cannot afford an attorney, one will be appointed for you. Do you understand these rights, as I've read them to you?"

There was a stunned silence for about 10 seconds while everyone absorbed his speech, then a wave of shocked murmurs rippled across the room behind him. He ignored all of it, his gaze never wavering from the face of his suspect. Whitmore was staring down at him with a stunned expression that was genuine shock, although he couldn't tell if the shock was at being accused or at being caught.

"Do you understand your rights Mr. Whitmore?"

His prompting finally elicited an affirmative nod from the

suspect and Sam gestured to the deputy on his right to put the handcuffs on. Without further ado, they led him from the room. The crowd, struggling to understand the sudden change in the situation, parting silently before them.

9:30 p.m.

The detective leaned across the brushed steel table in the interrogation room and looked closely at his prime suspect thinking that he would have fooled even the most hardened of cops with his protests of innocence. Sam wasn't fooled for a minute. Even the most innocent looking had a way of turning out to be capable of the most outrageous crimes.

He had learned that in his 20 years on the force in Kansas City; before he had retreated to this little town where supposedly nothing ever happened. This guy had motive, opportunity and the technical knowledge to have killed the Chief. Certainly, there were enough witnesses willing to make statements to corroborate motive. Access and know-how were also pretty solid since the Chief had been killed by somebody who knew enough medicine to replace the contents of the insulin vial with a dextrose solution. The Deputy Chief, who was also the station's lead EMT, certainly filled that bill nicely.

All the witnesses told the same story on that score; that Whitmore had clearly been through the Chief's desk in the past since he knew what was in it. Even more importantly, he didn't have an alibi for the time between the election and the murder.

Unfortunately, even with the circumstantial evidence pointing to him, there really wasn't any concrete proof that he did it. No fingerprints on the bottle (except the Chief of course) or the syringes and nobody had seen him near the bunk room or the Chief's office that night. Perhaps that was what was bothering him, the guy seems genuinely shocked that he was a suspect and really seemed to want to help find the killer.

If it was an act, it was a pretty good one. Still he had gotten convictions on nothing but circumstantial evidence in the past. If the circumstantial stuff was strong enough and the situation was one in which it was unlikely that there would ever be any true physical evidence, juries could be convinced on circumstances alone.

Leaning in closer, he looked at his suspect.

"Tell me again, where you were that evening after the election until about 11 o'clock."

"I went straight home after the election, I'm sure plenty of folks saw me leave, especially since I was slamming doors and cussing pretty loud on the way out. Anyway, I thought that the Chief had a heart attack, at least that's what the paper said. You guys keep saying that it was murder but nobody will say HOW he was murdered. If it wasn't his heart, what was it?"

"For now I'm not saying anything about that. I learned that the hard way when I was working in the city. If you to give away all the details of the case, screwballs come out of the woodwork, and it gives the real culprit that much more time to cover their tracks. Suffice it to say that he had to have been murdered by somebody with a pretty fair knowledge of medicine, somebody with enough of a grudge to commit murder and somebody with no alibi for the three hours between the election and his death."

"How am I supposed to defend myself against your accusations if I don't even know exactly WHAT I'm being accused of doing? I think maybe I need to have a lawyer present before we go any further."

"Now why would you say that? If, as you say, you didn't do anything wrong, what harm is there in answering my questions?"

"C'mon Detective, I'm not that naïve. I know that you can use anything I say against me, even if what I say is perfectly innocent. The truth has a way of getting twisted around."

"Too much TV Chief, I'm not the bad guy here."

"What did you say your name was detective? Who watches too much TV?"

"Yeah, I know. My real name is Samuel, but being a cop, everybody shortens it to Sam „cause they think it's funny. Before you ask, my folks never liked TV, I was named after my grandfather; and I've heard every joke you can possibly imagine so let's stick to the subject. Why did you kill the Chief?"

"I keep telling you, I didn't kill him. I'm not the bad guy either, but I can't prove it without knowing what I'm supposed to have done. Since you won't tell me, I want a lawyer here to make sure that things stay sane."

Sam looked at the man sitting across the table. Somehow, he really wanted to believe him. This really was beginning to feel like a bad TV show. Even the conversation felt like dialog from some 60's crime drama. On the other hand, lousy dialog doesn't make the situation any less real and nobody else had the motive this guy had. Even if he believed the guy was innocent, the DA was pressing him for somebody to prosecute and this guy was the best suspect they had. He wants a lawyer; the law says he gets a lawyer, nothing said they couldn't have a nice social chat before the lawyer showed up. He got up and opened the door to talk to the uniform in the hall.

"Guy wants his lawyer; get my cell phone off my desk, will you?"

Going back to the table, he sat down and leaned back in the chair, one hand resting casually on the table in front of him.

"While we wait for the phone, why don't we chat? Nothing to do with the murder of course, now that you've asked for your lawyer, I can't discuss that with you until he shows up. Who is your lawyer anyway?"

"I haven't needed one since the divorce and even that

was more of a formality than anything else. I guess I'll call my neighbor, Alex. Alex is the only lawyer I know well, certainly the only one I know well enough to call in the middle of the night like this."

"Does Alex have a last name?"

Before he could answer, the uniformed officer returned with the phone, handing it to the detective who in turn passed it across the table between them.

"Call your lawyer."

The call didn't last very long, he spent a couple of minutes talking to his neighbor and got a promise that help would arrive shortly along with an admonition not to say anything else until they were together.

The next 20 minutes were probably the longest of his life. Sitting across from the annoyed detective, trying not to fidget while refusing to respond to anything the other man said to him was nerve wracking. By the time Alex arrived, the detective was nearly apoplectic.

It was with considerable relief that he watched his 6 foot 2 inch, blond bombshell of a neighbor sweep majestically into the room. It was nearly midnight when she swept into the room, not a hair out of place. Even though it was late at night, she had taken the time to put on a peach silk suit with cream blouse and to pull her hair up into a French twist at the back of her head. It was amazing to watch her and really gratifying to see the detective's face when he caught his first sight of Alex.

It was obvious from his staggered expression that he had been expecting an Alexander rather than an Alexandra, especially an Alexandra that looked like she had just stepped out of a magazine centerfold and into the boardroom.

She took one quick look at the occupants of the room and rounded on the detective before he could react to her appearance.

"I want to talk to my client, ALONE detective. Right

now, before anybody says anything else."

The look she gave him would have withered a lesser man like grass in the desert. He had to give the detective credit for a fast recovery; he simply got up out of his chair and offered it to her.

"Of course... Counselor."

As she insinuated herself into the chair and he prepared to leave the room she looked up at him sweetly and smiled,

"Oh detective, please make sure the video and audio surveillance is turned off as soon as you leave the room, I assume you had them activated while questioning my client?"

Sam just stared for a moment before nodding affirmatively at her.

"Good. I'll want a copy of that tape detective, before we leave the station if you don't mind. Now, I would like some privacy to speak with my client."

FOUR

I stared at her in awe. I had never seen a more masterful put down in my life. It was amazing how she could handle men like the detective without even batting a lash. Alex and I had been neighbors for just under two years and were on fairly friendly terms, always getting along well, and helping each other out, what with adjoining yards and such. We'd never gotten to be more than just friends; but that didn't mean I hadn't had a thought or three in that direction over the years. It just never seemed to be the right moment to suggest anything more and we were both comfortable with the casual friendship that had evolved between us. Seeing her in her power mode made me aware once more that this was an incredibly attractive woman and one that could probably handle any stress, even that of being involved with a firefighter. Of course, the present really wasn't the time to dive into a relationship, but it certainly was something worth considering for the future; assuming that I didn't end up in a federal penitentiary someplace.

She turned to me and smiled before shaking her head in dismay.

"Ok James, suppose you tell me what the hell is going on? You call me up in the middle of the night and tell me YOU, of all people, have been arrested for murder? Who are you supposed to have killed and why do they think that you did it?"

I launched into the whole story, as I knew it. She already knew that Gus was dead; the whole town knew that and since almost everybody had attended the funeral just a few hours earlier, she was certainly no exception. I ran through what little I knew, including the fact that I had no idea, other than the apparent motive of our very public argument at the election, why the police thought I had killed him. I included a brief rendition of the interrogation up the point where I had asked for a lawyer.

"I'm glad you called me, I just wish you had done it a

bit sooner. People always fall for that line about not needing a lawyer if they haven't done anything wrong and it almost always ends up getting them into trouble. At least you don't seem to have said anything that will cause any problems. I'm not going to ask if you did it or not because I'm not all that confident that they stopped recording us."

She glanced sardonically at the two-way mirror on the wall.

"Or that they aren't still listening in on what is legally a confidential conversation. We'll save that part of the conversation for later, after we get you out of here."

Giving them the benefit of the doubt, she got up and went to the door to let the uniformed officer outside know that the detective could return.

"We have to observe the niceties, if only to keep things civil."

After Detective Gunne returned and took his seat across from them, she went on the offensive, and I found myself thinking, so much for the niceties.

"Suppose you tell us exactly what it is you're charging my client with, Detective? I know what the name of the charge is but you're going to have to do better than that, he has a right to know exactly what actions he is being accused of having performed. What evidence do you have that Mr. Whitmore is guilty of murder?"

"The details of the case that I'm about to tell you haven't been made public yet and we'd like to keep it that way for the moment. Chief Barnes was an insulin dependent diabetic, which was common knowledge. Laboratory tests found that his blood sugar at the time of death was 586 milligrams per deciliter. According to the Medical examiner, that is certainly high enough to have killed him."

He glared hard at me as he paused to let the information sink in...

Before he could continue, I broke in.

"Sure Gus was a diabetic. As you said, everybody knows that. He is been a Type 2 diabetic for years but he always kept it pretty well controlled. I'm surprised that he let it get that high, but high blood sugar in a diabetic is hardly indicative of murder."

"What we haven't told anyone is that somebody switched the contents of his insulin vial with a glucose solution."

I shot upright in my chair, staring at him.

"You're kidding right? I can't believe that anyone at the station would do such a thing... These are people who are dedicated to saving lives, not taking them."

Just as suddenly deflating, I let myself fall back in my chair.

"You realize what that means of course. The killer had to be somebody that knew how to make the switch without the Chief noticing any difference in the vial. It also had to be somebody who knew exactly where the Chief kept his kit and had access to the glucose and syringes."

Sam smiled slightly, "Yeah that is pretty much how we had it figured. Of course, you fit that description pretty well, in my opinion. It also had to be somebody with the motive to commit murder in the first place."

He looked over at Alex.

"You might want to advise your client not to be so helpful Counselor. There were a couple of dozen eyewitnesses at that election who have already given us statements regarding the blowup between the Chief and Mr. Whitmore here. That certainly corroborates his motive. He also seems to be the one with the most to gain from the Chief's death. Everybody involved acknowledges that with Gus Barnes out of the way, your client automatically becomes the Fire Chief, something he has tried to do for years if the historical records of the elections are any guide. As an experienced EMT, he has the knowledge of how to make the switch and the access to the various supplies needed to do it is available at the station. Only three people at the station have keys to the medication locker, your client is one of them. The Chief was the second one and the supply officer the third. It's a fairly safe bet that the Chief didn't do it and nobody seems to be able to find any motive for the supply officer. Means, motive, and opportunity, all point to Mr. Whitmore here. Not to mention the fact that he has no alibi for the three hours between the time he stormed out of the election and the time of death."

He paused dramatically and glanced at the folder lying open on the table in front of him, "Stormed out of the station, in a murderous rage, as one witness put it."

Alex looked disgusted,

"In other words, you have some circumstantial evidence that seems to point to my client as a suspect, but no actual evidence, isn't that right detective Gunne? Do you have any hard evidence that points to my client? Anything at all?"

She glared at the detective for a moment, while he fidgeted with the documents on the table in front of him, before turning to put a hand on my arm.

"I didn't think so. My client and I will be leaving now. I suggest that the next time you arrest somebody, you actually have some evidence first."

She stood up and then turned to look down at me because I hadn't moved at all.

"Come on, we don't have anything else to say to these gentlemen."

"Actually, I have a question for the detective, if that's OK."

"I really don't think you should say anything else at this point but tell me your question."

She leaned down so that her ear was near my lips and

I whispered to her. She sat back down and looked at me as if she was impressed (I hoped she was anyway).

"Go ahead, and ask your question, I expect to be fascinated by the answer".

"What makes you think that the insulin could only have been switched after the election? Why couldn't it have been done any time before that?"

Sam sat up straighter in his chair, goggling, "What do you mean? When do YOU think it happened?"

"I have no idea when it happened, but there isn't really any reason that it had to be just before he died. There isn't any reason why it couldn't have been done days or even a couple of weeks beforehand. Gus always kept a spare vial of insulin in the butter compartment of the refrigerator in the station kitchen, just in case the one in his kit ran out while he was there. Anybody who ever walked into that kitchen had access to it, and pretty much every regular member knew it was there. There are plenty of times when the station is basically empty; anyone who had a door code could have done it anytime in recent days."

Sam fell back in his chair with a dumbfounded expression on his face and Alex was practically smirking at him.

"Thank you James, I think we have done enough of his work for him now, I suggest that we leave Element's finest to get on with their investigation."

"Detective", she purred, "Do let us know if we can do anything else for you but remember that anything else you have to say to my client, you can say through me."

She rose gracefully and looked at both of us with a bit of amusement.

"Coming James?"

FIVE

My God, she was magnificent! I think I was probably half way to being in love with her at that point. I can't recall ever having seen anybody handle the police so smoothly. The only side of Alex I had ever seen before was the friendly neighbor; tonight she had outdone herself as my lawyer. From the peach silk business suit and sleek, pinned up hair, to the absolute assurance of every move and word, she had radiated power and a confidence in me that I had never even had in myself. I remember being absolutely dumbstruck when she swept into that dingy interrogation room. It was like somebody had opened the door and let in a hurricane. That poor detective had never stood a chance against her and she had known it from the start.

As I walked with her out to her car, she leaned over and whispered to me not to say anything until we got back to the house. As a result, the 5 minute drive was silent. I spent most of it just looking at her, wondering if I had really known her at all. That night she seemed to be somebody I had never seen before. I liked what I saw. I liked it a lot. Because I was letting my mind wander down a totally out of context path, I was caught by surprise when she pulled the car into her driveway and turned to look at me.

"I think we need to talk about a few things right now. Come inside and I will get us both some coffee."

The last time I had been in her house (in fact the only time that I could recall) was to deal with a bird that had managed to fly in through an open window. There really hadn't been much time to pay attention to what things looked like. Then my pager had gone off just about the time we had managed to get the exhausted sparrow back out the window. This time I paused to take a good look around. I think the perfect word for her style is sensuous; everything appeared to be about comfort, all warm colors, and soft textures. It was so at odds with her appearance and the take charge manner she had used at the police station that I had to pause to let my mind adjust. I followed as she led the way to the kitchen took a seat at the table while she pressed the start button on the coffee maker.

"James, I will defend you either way, if you want me to, but I need to know if you did it. I didn't ask at the station because I don't trust them not to be listening in, I also don't trust them not to have bugged my car. I doubt it, but with a murder charge, it doesn't pay to take chances. I don't think they had time to do anything here at the house though. Besides, I asked Martha across the street to call my cell if anybody came to either of our houses while I was gone. You know how she is; she never sleeps and she watches everything that happens on this street. Since my cell never rang, I think it's safe to assume we are OK here. For now though, I need the truth before we go any further. Did you kill Gus Barnes?"

I wasn't sure whether to laugh or be offended that she asked but I guess it makes sense, a lawyer has to know what they are dealing with in order to know what to do.

"Of course I didn't do it. Look Alex, I know that everyone thinks I was angry enough to have done it, but I wasn't really. I was just upset about the way his supporters were pushing about Sara's death. It still hurts that she is gone and I just wasn't ready to deal with their ugly insinuations. I would never have hurt Gus though. Vengeance isn't my style."

"Good. You do realize that I had to ask, right?"

I nodded in agreement.

"Now there is something I need to tell you, I haven't done many criminal cases, it isn't my area of specialty. I mostly do corporate and real estate law, with the occasional divorce thrown in to pay the bills. If it comes down to a real legal battle, I will understand if you want to call in somebody with more background in criminal defense. On the other hand, at this point, I don't think that they have a case against you that would stand up in court anyway. I just want to you to know so that you understand the risks."

I was actually more relieved by her honesty than I was concerned by her lack of experience. I had seen her in action and if she handled juries and judges the way she had that detective, I was in good hands.

"As you said, I don't think they have a case against me, especially since I didn't do it. However, I'm glad you told me. Regardless of your experience, I prefer working with somebody I already know. I've got to tell you though that I don't have much money, working for the phone company pays okay, but it will never get anybody rich."

She looked at me and smiled.

"Let's just take things as they come for now. I think that it might be over at this point because unless they can come up with physical evidence, they really don't have enough to try you on a murder charge. If they do come up with some evidence, it will have to be pretty rock solid since you have already made it clear that almost anybody with access to the station could have done it."

By that point, it was already way too late to try to get any sleep for the night since it was already 2 a.m. so we just sat in her kitchen and talked the rest of the night. Alex isn't a member of the fire department and so I had to tell her the entire story of the election, the arguments, and the mudslinging that had gone on, and which were the reason everyone thought I had killed Gus. She in turn asked me a lot of questions that the police had never bothered to ask. Questions like, did I actually have an affair with the Chief's wife.

It wasn't an episode that I was particularly proud of, but it had happened. The affair had started shortly after Sara left me and during the time when Gus had been traveling a lot on business. To be honest with Gus out of town and me in the middle of a divorce, Carla and I hadn't been particularly discreet about the whole thing. The end result was that Gus had found out about the affair. As soon as that happened, Carla had ended it. It hadn't been a true love kind of affair as much as just two lonely people who needed someone.

She also asked about Sara's death and that was a lot harder to discuss. By the time we had finished dredging through my painful past it was almost sunrise and I was exhausted. I knew I really should've tried to get some sleep but I also knew that as my lawyer Alex needed to know the whole story and all the details if she ended up having to defend me. Besides, I really enjoyed her company and it was probably very good to finally talk some of that stuff out. She was a really good listener.

I got back home just in time to take a shower and change clothes for work. Of course going to work was the last thing I wanted to do between having gotten no sleep and knowing that the entire town was probably talking about my arrest the previous day. I knew that it was important to show my face so that people understood that the police had let me go. It also never hurts to be out there to tell your side of the story instead of letting rumors be encouraged by your absence. Having decided that I headed to the office although not without a good deal of apprehension, most of which appeared to be entirely justified since a lot of people seemed kind of shocked to see me walking about the streets as a free man.

I think it just about drove me crazy that morning because I've lived in this town all my life. These people have known me since the day I was born and all of a sudden, they were looking at me as if I was the leading villain in a horror flick. I walked into the office and all conversation stopped. Nobody seemed to know quite what to say or how to react to me being there. I probably hadn't been at my desk more than a couple of minutes when my boss asked to see me privately. I had this horrible feeling I knew what was coming and I was right.

"James I want you to know that I don't believe for one minute that you could've killed anyone but I have to lookout for the reputation of this company. Because of that I don't think it's a good idea for you to be here, at least until these charges have been cleared up. I hope you understand that this isn't personal; this is just business and I have to follow directions from my superiors."

I looked at him and had this hysterical urge to laugh even though I knew it was a serious situation. Here was a man who claimed to believe completely in my innocence, but his body language said just the opposite. He sat on the far side of his desk from me, something he never does; Bill is more likely to sit on the corner of the desk nearest to you when he talks to you. His entire body was rigid and he didn't seem to be able to look me directly in the eye, another thing he doesn't usually have a problem with.

"Bill, I suggest you check with the police before you say anything else that either one of us will regret. The charges have been dropped, no bail, no pending hearing, nothing. Basically, it was all for nothing because I didn't do anything wrong and I was able to prove that to their satisfaction last night. If the police believe me, why are you having so much trouble?"

I watched him shift around in his chair for a bit before continuing.

"However, I'll make it easy on you; I'm tired so I think I'll take a personal day today. That'll give you time to get the story straight and me time to get some sleep."

He at least had the grace to look confused and a bit embarrassed by my outburst.

"But then what was all that about after the funeral yesterday, when the police claimed you were under arrest?"

"Perhaps it was just a bit of confusion, or perhaps the police and I are working together to throw the real killer off-track so they will make a mistake, or perhaps they just screwed up. Take your pick."

"Are you still a suspect?"

By that time, I was starting to get a little fed up with the whole conversation but I knew that losing my temper probably wouldn't help the situation at all.

"No more so than every other member of the fire department."

I got up and opened the office door. As I walked out into the main office area, I turned back and said, just loud enough for everyone to hear.

"As of 11 o'clock last night when I left the police station they had absolutely no idea who killed Gus. But they knew it wasn't me."

With that parting shot, I grabbed my stuff from my desk and headed home to get some sleep, only stopping at the last moment to turn and look at Bill down the length of the room and say brightly, "See you on Monday morning".

The whole situation was just ridiculous and I really wanted to just sort of walk down Main Street shouting out loud, "I didn't do it, okay? I didn't do it!"

Instead, I just went home and crawled into bed.

SIX

Immediately after Whitmore and his lawyer left the station, Sam had grabbed a couple of uniforms and an evidence technician and sent them back down to the fire department in search of fresh evidence. The first stop was the kitchen to check the refrigerator for a vial of insulin. There wasn't one and there was no point in trying to fingerprint the refrigerator. After almost a week, any fingerprints would be useless because any number of people could have opened the refrigerator during that time.

Pretty much the same could be said for any evidence that they might find at the station so the next stop should have been James Whitmore's house. Unfortunately, that would require a warrant, which he didn't have yet since nobody had been able to find Judge Wells.

Not being able to do much else at the moment, he sent a deputy over to keep an eye on the Whitmore place, while he went to catch a few hours of overdue rest. Once somebody managed to track down the judge and talk him into issuing a warrant, they could continue the investigation. In the meantime, there really wasn't very much he could accomplish, so getting some sleep seemed a reasonable thing to do.

It didn't seem like he had been asleep very long, although his clock said he had gotten about 4 ½ hours in, when one of the deputies returned with the search warrant. He dressed quickly, and armed with the warrant (he figured the stacked blond lawyer would skin him alive if he tried to enter the house without one) they headed over to the Whitmore place.

They parked on the street out front of a tidy little cream colored two-story cape bungalow. The lawn was the kind of lush green perfectly manicured grass that he usually associated with golf courses and professional gardeners. It made him wonder how a man with a full time job, who spent most of his free time at the fire station, managed to have such a perfect yard. The house was just as tidy. Probably about 40 years old, it certainly showed some signs of its age, but the siding was bright and clean, as were the fairly new looking double - hung windows. The covered front porch sported a swinging bench, suspended by shiny chains and accompanied by a small table on the far end which looked perfect for supporting a tall cold drink on hot summer afternoons. All-in-all he thought it made a lovely postcard. He walked up the steps onto the porch and rang the front door.

Whitmore showed up at the door barefoot, dressed in sweatpants and a tee-shirt, both emblazoned with EMT down the left side in bright yellow letters. When Sam handed him the warrant and demanded entry to the house he seemed more annoyed than upset.

"Shouldn't you have come here looking for evidence BEFORE you arrested me on suspicion of murder?"

"Yeah, I should have but the judge took a couple of days off. We had to track him down before we could even try convincing him to issue a search warrant. Turns out, he'd gone fishing up on Miller's Creek, and you can only get there on horseback or on foot. I had to send a deputy up there to get the judge's signature. That is one thing I miss about working in a big city. You could always find a judge when you needed one. Anyway, we're here now, and as you can see that warrant gives us the right to search your home for any evidence related to this case. Please step outside and don't come back in until we give you permission."

The inside of his house was more like what one would expect from a bachelor. While there weren't any old pizza boxes lying around; there was a pile of unfolded laundry heaped on the sofa and at least one day's worth of dishes in the sink. Even so, Whitmore was a better housekeeper than Sam.

Sam and the evidence technician went through the house, opening doors and cabinets; pulling out drawers and peering at the contents. Unfortunately, there didn't seem to be anything incriminating that they could find. Either it wasn't there in the first place or Whitmore had already disposed of it. Unfortunately, there wasn't any way to tell which one was the right answer.

While they were inside, rifling through the contents of his house, James walked next door to get his lawyer. The pair was waiting for him on the front step when he came out.

"I trust you've satisfied your curiosity now? Or do you intend to continue to harass my client?"

"I've seen what I needed to see for now. Just don't be planning any out-of-town vacations in the near future."

Reluctant to stand on the front sidewalk and enter into a battle of wits with the extraordinarily attractive lawyer, Sam motioned to the evidence technician and deputy and they all headed back to the car. The next stop would be the Barnes residence.

When they got to the house, Carla was awake. Dressed a pair of jeans and one of her husband's long sleeve shirts, she was just sitting on the sofa staring off into space, her arms wrapped around a pillow. When they told her that they had released James Whitmore and were now pursuing other leads she seemed pretty relieved which made Gus wonder. He would have thought that she would be upset to know that they no longer had a key suspect in her husband's murder but instead she seemed glad that their primary suspect had been set free. It was then that he remembered somebody saying that part of the argument preceding the murder had been about her having an affair with James Whitmore sometime in the past. In his mind, it was just one more reason to believe that the man was guilty. Perhaps the motive had been less about becoming Chief and more about stealing the Chief's wife. He would have to think about that little more, but it was certainly something to stash in his mental files about this case.

At his request Carla led the way out to the garage and showed the detective the small refrigerator where Gus kept all of his spare insulin as a general rule.

Gingerly, he used the tip of his pen to pry the refrigerator door open just in case there were any fingerprints on it. Inside were three vials of insulin.

"I probably should have thrown those out but it's just so hard to bring myself to get rid of anything connected with Gus. Do you really think that any of these have anything to do with Gus's death?"

Sam instructed the technician to take the vials and saw them placed in an evidence bag.

"No way to know at this stage but we will test them all and see what they tell us. In the meantime can you tell me if there are any other diabetic supplies here in the house that belonged to Gus or if he kept any insulin in places other than here or the station?"

"Well, certainly the rest of his supplies; syringes, glucometer, test strips, etc. are here at the house. He usually kept everything here except for the kit that he carried most of the time. I'm not really sure what it is your looking for detective. Perhaps if you give me some idea I could give you a better answer"

"To be perfectly honest Mrs. Barnes I'm not sure exactly what it is I expect to find. Anything out of the ordinary or out of place might give us some indicator of exactly what happened and more importantly, when it happened. If you would please, show me exactly where all these various items were kept it would be very useful. Also, let me know if anything looks out of place or out of the ordinary. I'm also going to need a list of anyone who had access to your house or to these supplies. Do you happen to know when your husband picked up these files from the pharmacy and which pharmacy he got them from?"

"Well, he didn't actually pick the supplies up from a physical pharmacy. Normally all of his medical supplies came from the VA through their mail-order pharmacy system. He would notify them a week or two before he was going to run out and they would process a refill and mail it to him. I think he received the last package a couple weeks ago but I'm not really sure. I would have expected there to be four vials at this point instead of just three. When I get a chance I will check and see if I can figure out exactly when they arrived."

"Please do that. Can you think of anyone besides yourself and Gus that might have known these supplies were here and had access to the house in the time between when they arrived and when he died?"

Carla tipped her head and looked at him thoughtfully.

"Gosh detective I'm really not sure. It depends, I suppose, on exactly when the supplies arrived. A lot of people stop by on a fairly regular basis to discuss various fire station issues, to discuss election strategy, to talk about what's stressing them or upsetting them, all of that kind of goes with the territory of being the Fire Chief. I can think of a dozen people who've been here the last two weeks. What I can't think of is a reason why any one of them might have wanted to hurt Gus."

"Mrs. Barnes, why did Gus keep his insulin out here in the garage and not in the refrigerator in the kitchen? It seems a bit odd to me."

"It's really not as strange as it might seem Mr. Gunne. As you can see, the only things in this little refrigerator are his insulin and cans of diet soda. He preferred to keep his insulin away from food that might contaminate the containers by getting on the top of the vials. Even though he was generally pretty careful about using alcohol to wipe them off before he drew his insulin into the syringe, he preferred to keep the vials as clean as possible anyway. The cans are sealed and not likely to contaminate anything. Just good sanitation basically."

After a few more questions about whether or not she had noticed anything unusual in the last couple of weeks, Sam elicited a promise that she would check on when they received the insulin shipment. She also promised to write down a list for him of everyone that she could remember as having been in the house since the time of the shipment as well as when they were there, approximately how long they stayed, if she knew, and whether or not they had been left alone at any time.

She didn't seem very happy about it and that bothered him a bit but perhaps she was just concerned at the idea of thinking about a killer having been in her house without her knowing it. It would certainly make most people uneasy.

After leaving the Barnes residence Sam stopped by the fire station to have another look around and try to get a feel for what had happened to the Chief.

When he arrived at the station the truck bay door was open and the ambulance and the engine were both gone. There was nobody around. With some disgust, he realized that it was probably pretty common that they left the door open when they went on an emergency call. It was a little disconcerting to realize that the whole town had access to the station and anyone could've been the killer.

What a wonderful situation he thought, the pool of suspects just increased from the members of the fire station to virtually any person in town.

SEVEN

After the detective left the house, Carla sat down and tried to write the list that he had asked for of people who had been by the House recently. The more she thought the longer the list grew. There were members of the church choir who had met to plan a bake sale last week, the station chaplain, a Boy Scout leader who had wanted to arrange for some of the boys to spend time at the station earning a merit badge. James had stopped by to discuss some new NFPA regulation; the station computer committee had met at the house two days before Gus died about whether to buy a new computer for the front office. The list just seemed to grow and grow.

It was hard to imagine anybody on the list wanting to hurt Gus, and somehow she just couldn't picture James doing it no matter how hard she tried. It just didn't make sense; she had never known James to intentionally hurt anyone in any way. He had even taken all the blame for their affair himself to avoid causing her any more pain than necessary when they had ended it. She wondered if the detective were aware of her history with James and if that had anything to do with them choosing him as a suspect. She hoped not because she found it easier to believe that the chaplain did it than James.

After checking through the phone record of last month's calls, she found the call to the VA that Gus had made to order his diabetes supplies. It had been three weeks ago at the end of June and that meant that the supplies had probably arrived 14 or 15 days ago based on past experience in shipping time. She went back and revisited the list to make sure that she had gotten as many names as possible going back the whole two weeks.

When she was done, she decided to drop the information off at the station for the detective. Getting dressed she wondered how James was doing after the public humiliation that the police had caused him at the funeral the day before. Deciding to check on him, she called his house and left a message on his answering machine.

"James its Carla. I just wanted to check and see how you were doing. Detective Gunne was just here and said that they had released you. I was really glad to hear it because I know that you would never have harmed Gus. Please don't be a stranger; I've a feeling we were both going to need all the friends we can get for a while."

Just saying it made her feel better although she wasn't quite sure why. Still, it didn't matter; she had just wanted James to know that somebody in town believed he was innocent. She knew full well how small towns could be and this one was no different. Everyone knows everyone else's business and there is always somebody willing to share dirt or see the worst in other people. Until this whole thing got cleared up once and for all there were going to be people who believed that James was guilty. For that fact even once the real killer was caught and convicted there would still be some that expressed doubt about his innocence. She hated to think that she had any part in causing that.

It felt so strange to leave the house without writing a note to let her husband know where she would be. After 23 years of marriage, that habit was going to be really hard to break, right along with a lot of other little habits and routines that are part of a successful marriage. It had been a successful marriage, aside from that one interlude with James when Gus had been spending all of his time at the station or out of town and she had felt ignored. It hadn't lasted long, once he realized what was happening he had made a real effort to be at home more. Sometimes that meant having people from the station come to the house to talk to him, but that was okay because it still gave them more time together. After that, their marriage had been pretty strong and she had reveled in the time they spent together.

She stopped by the station and dropped off the papers

with the desk sergeant, asking him to make sure that Detective Gunne received them. Walking back out the front door of the station she suddenly realized that she had no idea where to go or what to do with her time now that she was alone. On a normal day, she would have stopped by the store and picked up something for dinner, perhaps going over to visit Muriel at the library for a little while, and then gone home to make sure dinner was ready when Gus got there.

Somewhat at a loss, she decided that she could at least go visit Muriel. Maybe she'd even find something to read, she would certainly have enough free time to catch up on her reading now. Grocery shopping just didn't seem reasonable at the moment and half the town seems to have stopped by the day before and delivered food so she really didn't need to cook tonight. Oh, but the days were going to be empty.

She walked up the two blocks to the library trying to let the sun soak in and warm her along the way. When she got there, Muriel was busy with a group of children from the elementary school. They were learning the Dewey decimal system but they didn't seem very impressed by it. She wandered over to the fiction section and browsed through the titles for awhile, trying to see if any of her favorite authors have written anything new recently. Nothing really seemed interesting. Eventually she found herself back at the front desk just in time to see Muriel ushering the children out the front door and back to their waiting teacher.

After spending about an hour making small talk with Muriel, she finally gave it up and decided that she just wasn't feeling very social at the moment. They'd been friends for years and she knew Muriel would understand because she was also a widow. A widow. It wasn't a word she ever thought would apply to her. For some reason in her mind, a widow was a bent a little old lady who had been alone for years, gray hair, grown kids that don't live nearby, etc... A widow wasn't supposed to be an attractive woman in her mid-40s.

Everything seemed so surreal and she knew that she was just sort of drifting along without any particular purpose or destination. It was a surprise when she realized that she had walked over to James's house without really intending to. For a minute, she just stood there looking at the house wondering why she was there. After all her husband had only been dead a few days, and yet she going over to the house of the man that the police claimed was his killer. Of course, that was bullshit and she knew it. Perhaps it was just that James had been her best friend for a while and right now, she really needed a best friend to talk to. For sure, she really didn't want to go back to the house alone just yet.

Finally working herself up to walking towards his front door, she was a bit taken back when she saw Alex Kincaid coming from his house. She knew that Alex lived right next door but she just hadn't expected to see her there. Alex looked up, saw her, and headed towards her with a smile.

"Carla, I'm so sorry about Gus. He was a very special man and I know he was devoted to you."

They worked their way through the requisite polite phrases and condolences in very short order after which there was a slightly awkward silence between them. It was broken when Carla asked Alex how James was doing.

"Well, it's like you might expect; having been accused of murder in front of half the town and then released for lack of evidence. He tried going to work earlier today and it was so blatantly obvious that people are uncomfortable around him and he just decided to come home. It's going to be rough for a while with everybody suspecting him the way they do. I'm a little surprised to see you on his front doorstep this afternoon though."

"I wanted to see how he was doing, I don't believe for a second that he would hurt Gus. I know what you mean about people in this town not having much faith in him; I've heard a couple comments myself. Mostly I wanted to stop by and let him know that I didn't believe the charges were true. He is going to need friends in the days to come until this all gets cleared up and I wanted him to know that I'm is still his friend just has Gus was."

"That's nice. I know he would appreciate the sentiment. On the other hand, you coming here might give those gossips that are spreading the story and the accusations even more ammunition. Plenty of folks know that you and James had an affair several years ago. Some of them with their minds in the gutter might think that you and James conspired to get rid of Gus so that you could be together. I know it's a silly thing for them to think, but there are always those willing to think the worst of everyone around them. Under the circumstances it might be best not to throw any more fuel on the fire for a while, if you know what I mean."

It was awfully hard to keep the insult and the fury that it caused out of her expression and her voice when she responded to the innuendo from Alex but she manage it, barely.

"Are you trying to tell me that just stopping by to voice my support for him could actually make his situation worse? I don't believe it, this is ridiculous! Am I just supposed to shun him in an effort to help him? That's not exactly my style. I prefer to stand up for my friends in times of trouble."

"Oh no, that's not what I meant at all. I didn't mean to upset you, honestly. I'm certainly not trying to tell you what to do. James is your friend and you want him to know that you don't believe the charges against him. I agree he needs to know that, I think you're coming here to tell him is admirable. What I'm saying is that there is more than enough suspicion already and you know as well as I do that the diehard gossips will find something negative in the most innocent of situations. This is murder, hardly an innocent situation. Even though you and I are certain that James is innocent, if we really want to help him, we won't do anything that might give the gossips something more to speculate on. I'm saying this not only as James's friend, and your friend, but also as his lawyer. As his lawyer is my job to look out for his best interests in relation to this case. I'm trying to do that."

"This is unbelievable. First, somebody kills my husband and now I'm not even allowed to talk to my friends. I don't understand what this world is coming to, I really don't. Fine, great, whatever. Do me one favor would you? Next time you talk to James, please tell them that I stopped by and that I believe he is innocent. Would you do that for me please?"

"Of course I will. I'm really only trying to do what's best for James and for you, you do realize that don't you?"

She had to agree, even though she hated to. She had known Alex for a couple of years and knew that she was a good lawyer. As much as she hated to admit it, under the circumstances Alex was probably right. Feeling even more depressed than she had been when leaving the library, Carla headed back to her too quiet house. As she walked back up the street she didn't notice the curtains twitching at the Cornell House across the street, where Gladys Cornell had gleefully taken note of her presence and of what appeared to be a less than friendly encounter between the two women on James's front sidewalk.

EIGHT

Alex had stopped by about two-thirty to see how I was doing and ask a couple of more questions about what was probably involved in the switching of the insulin. I guess it was mostly just so she understood enough about what had happened to Gus to be able to counter any additional questions or charges that came up. It made sense, after all how can she defend me   against something she   doesn't even understand.

I explained the physical process of using a syringe to first pump air into the vial, and then draw the insulin out. The reverse procedure would then be used to push the glucose solution in and draw out excess air to equalize the pressure. It isn't hard to do but it did occur to me that the standard insulin syringes, which are very small, couldn't be used to do it very easily. Generally, the largest insulin syringes only hold 1 cc of liquid but the vials normally contain 10 cc; so it would take a lot of effort to empty and refill a vial using a syringe that only held 1/10 of the amount needed. Of course, I don't suppose that really helps any since larger syringes are available at the station. Still, perhaps the police were looking for the wrong size syringe as they searched for clues. I would have to remember to mention that to detective Gunne the next time I spoke to him.

Alex didn't stay long; we were both still pretty tired from the stress and lack of sleep from the night before. Shortly after she left I heard voices out front. I twitched back the curtains from my upstairs bedroom window and peaked down to see Alex and Carla talking on the front sidewalk. I couldn't hear what was being said but Carla looked pretty annoyed. I really wanted to go down and talk to her but I was afraid that she would tell me that she believed the accusations against me. I really didn't think I could stand it, so I took the chicken way out and let Alex handle it. Alex would tell me if it were important.

I watched the two of them arguing for a few minutes, and

eventually Carla stalked away down the street. More depressed than I ever remember feeling in my whole life, I turned and headed for the shower. A nice hot soapy shower might not help, but it certainly couldn't hurt at the moment and it seemed to be just about all I had energy left to do. Nothing was normal anymore. One of my best friends was dead, murdered by person or persons unknown. I had spent most of last night at the police station being interrogated, after being hauled away in handcuffs in front of a roomful of people I had known most of my life. To make it all even worse, one of the people I cared about most of the world apparently believed that I could be guilty of such a thing.

With no idea what to do next or how to get out of the situation I found myself in, I pretty much just stood in the shower letting the hot water soothe away some of the knotted muscles. After getting out of the shower, I put on a pair of sweatpants and a T-shirt and headed back downstairs to do something about dinner. Not really being in the mood to cook or being very hungry I settled for just a beer, grabbed a pad of paper and a pencil and sat down on the sofa to make some notes and try and figure stuff out.

I started off by writing down everything I knew about what had happened to Gus. Unfortunately, it wasn't a very long list. I knew when he died and thanks to Detective Gunne, I knew how he died. That's about it. I had no idea who might have wanted him dead; it just didn't make sense that anyone from the station would have done it. I had no idea when they could have made the switch. With no motive, no time, and about 100 people with access to the station, there just didn't seem to be any way to solve it. Unfortunately, that kind of left me holding the bag; since the police had publicly accused me of the crime there were going to be people that believed it. If I couldn't find a way to prove who had really done it, or at least to help the police figure it out, it would always be hanging over my head, and there would always be people willing to point their finger at me as a murderer.

"Damn it! This is ridiculous, what the hell am I

supposed to do now? I hate this and I don't see any way out of it".

My outburst was punctuated by the half- empty beer can hitting the wall on the other side of the living room and splattering on the plaque that I received from Gus at the installation dinner the first year that I was elected as Deputy Chief. "I've got to get out of this house and do something. I just don't know what."

Heading upstairs to my bedroom I dug my sneakers from under the bed, I hauled them on without bothering to put on socks first and headed for the front door. When all else fails, get physically active. It had worked well for me for a lot of years so there was no reason why it shouldn't help now. I ran hard for several miles, working up a good sweat and burning off some of the adrenaline that had been building up during my outburst. I had made it all away through the south end of town and past a couple of local farms before I finally eased up a bit and turned back towards the house. I was about halfway back home when I decided instead to go by the station to make sure things were running smoothly there. I dropped back into an easy jogging pace and made the remaining mile to the station only moderately winded.

I got to the station just as the alarm tones sounded for an ambulance call. I grabbed my turnout gear from where it was hanging on a rack that stretched across the back of the equipment bay, dragged it on over my sweats, and climbed into the right front seat of the ambulance just as Chuck and Larry showed up. The right front seat is where the officer typically sits so that they can use the radio, read maps, and leave the driver free to navigate the vehicle.

Larry was a driver for the station and generally didn't get involved in patient care; Chuck was a seasoned EMT, having been a member of the station for more than a dozen years. Both of them seemed awfully surprised to see me there which didn't really make me feel any better. It didn't really matter though because in my book, the patient comes first and everything else comes second. It doesn't matter what else is going on in my life or at the station; the patient is what counts. It seemed to me that Larry was hesitating to climb into the driver's seat and it took me a second to realize that it was because of me. I couldn't let this continue or it would get completely out of control.

"Larry, let's go. The patient can't wait forever."

He climbed in and sat gingerly behind the wheel looking at me out of the corner of his eye.

"Damn it Larry either drive or get the hell out of the vehicle, the call is for chest pains and I will be damned if I will let the patient die because you can't decide if you want to be in the same vehicle with me or not. If you're not going to drive, then get out and make room for somebody who will. I won't tolerate a risk to the patient for the sake of your sensibilities, so make up your mind right now which way it's going to be."

The engine roared to life and the ambulance shot out of the bay as he stomped on the gas. It was probably a really good thing that the sirens were going as we headed down the road, it made conversation almost impossible. I was pretty steamed at that point so not talking was probably a good idea. An ambulance isn't the most comfortable ride around, but they are built to handle almost anything you can put them through. Not to mention that there are about two dozen compartments full of stuff that has to be properly secured to avoid having it scattered all over the road if you take a sharp corner.

It only took a couple minutes to get to the location of the call which turned out to be the home of Michelle Gantt, a life member of the station. Since Michelle was at the door waving to us urgently, the victim was probably her husband Bill. Sure enough, when Chet and I got inside the house we found Bill on the floor grey, rigid, and sweaty. Michelle had probably put him there because even though she wasn't an EMT she knew enough to recognize the signs of a heart attack and to know that we would need the patient on a hard flat surface if

CPR was required.

Any surprise or reluctance that Chuck might have felt about working with me disappeared in the urgency of taking care of Bill; which was probably a good thing because I wasn't sure how much more I could have handled at that point. We split the tasks involved in initial assessment in order to get things done as efficiently as possible. Chuck took vital signs while I got the oxygen going, which seemed to help Bill a little bit. I unpacked and set up to monitor while he placed electrodes on Bills chest so that we could see what his heart was doing. A quick look at the EKG told us both that we had better get Bill into definitive care pretty darn fast.

We loaded him up on the gurney and made him as comfortable as possible for transport to the hospital. I remember thinking, God, don't let him die, the last thing I need right now is to have another person die in close proximity to me. I know that sounds a bit self-centered and callous, and the truth is I really didn't want him to die for reasons that had nothing to do with me and everything to do with the fact that I had known Michelle and Bill most of my life. It was just the result of the accumulated stresses of the past week. Let's be realistic, after the accusations before the election about Sara and the arrest for purportedly murdering Gus; the last thing I needed was to be associated with someone else's death regardless of whether it was my fault for not.

By the time we got him to the ER and got him turned over to the medical staff he seemed to be doing a little better and Michelle was genuinely grateful that we had been there to help.

As we were collecting and packing our gear to get ready to leave and they were preparing to take him up to the Cardiac Care Unit; she gave me a hug and whispered in my ear,

"Thank you for taking care of Bill, I didn't believe for a single second that you could have hurt anyone. Especially not Gus. Lots of us don't believe it, so you keep your spirits up."

Man that felt good. I was used to having people say thank you at the end of an ambulance run but this time it meant so much more because of her faith in me. We finished collecting our gear and stowing it in the ambulance. It takes a while to put everything away in an ambulance, because there are about two dozen compartments, each with their own function, and every item has to go back in exactly the right place so that the next crew can find it when they need it without having to hunt. For the moment, we just got everything back in the box, which is what we call the patient care area on the backend of the ambulance, so we could get back to the station and do it properly. I got out and stood behind the ambulance directing Larry, while he backed it in. Once it was parked in the bay, the three of us set to work cleaning it up and putting everything back in its proper place. The sheets on the gurney had to be changed, any gear used had to be cleaned and inspected, the level of oxygen remaining in the tank needed to be checked, so that we wouldn't run low in the middle of the next call.

While we were working on the ambulance a couple of the more obnoxious, and junior, members decided to cause a scene. Even worse, they didn't have the guts to confront me face-to-face, at least not at first. Apparently, it was much more fun to stand over to the side and make snide comments just barely loud enough to be heard while we cleaned up and restocked.

"I can't believe he has the gall to be here after what he did."

"I'm surprised any patients allowed him to touch them",

"It really would be best if he resigned, the station really doesn't need any more scandal right now".

Chuck, Larry, and I worked silently to prep the ambulance for whatever the next call might be, choosing to ignore them as much as possible. Eventually though Chuck had had enough and headed towards them. Now, Chuck isn't the biggest guy you've ever seen, in fact at 5'4", he is definitely the shortest EMT in the station, so it was pretty amazing when he managed to back these two idiots up against the wall as he told them off. Here he was this little bitty guy who probably weighs 120 pounds (soaking wet with a beer in each hand) facing down these two yahoos who had been football players in high school.

If the situation hadn't been so tense, it would've been the funniest thing I've ever seen. Diminutive Chuck standing right in front of them, his feet spread and his hands on his hips as he dressed them down. I'll probably never figure out how he managed to look down his nose at them while looking up at them. He never even raised his voice. He just used that tone that high school principals have perfected over the centuries, the one that makes you feel about as useful and intelligent as a bug.

"I don't know what game you fools are trying to play but you had better stop it right now. James has been a member of this station longer than you have been alive and he is certainly better known and better respected than either of you. If you think for one minute that he could've actually hurt Gus or anybody else then you don't know a thing about him. I've never known anybody more dedicated to helping people and saving lives than James Whitmore, so you can take your sly comments and your paranoid suspicions and get out. At least he is here when the tones go out which is more than I can say for you two idiots. So if you're not going to be useful than you'd better not be around."

I just stood there and stared at Chuck. After he finished dressing them down he sauntered back over to the ambulance, looked up at me, and muttered, "Morons", before going back to working on the ambulance.

I looked over at Larry and raised my eyebrows in surprise when he shook his head in disgust.

"Damn young fools, it's no wonder Gus was so adamant about them not being ready to be officers. Can you imagine either of them as a Sergeant or Lieutenant?"

The thought sent shudders down my spine.

By the time we were done cleaning up and restocking, I was feeling a whole lot better about things in general. It was awfully nice to know that I still had friends after everything that had happened in the past 24 hours. Even though there were some people that believed I was guilty, or at least were willing to seize the moment in order to get me out of their hair, there also seemed to be plenty who were willing to stand by me. I suppose that a murder in a small town is the kind of thing that tends to polarize the population. That polarization has to be even worse when the primary suspect is somebody local.

I stuck around the station for a while, just to enjoy the camaraderie of people who no longer seemed to regard me as sitting someplace near the right hand of the Devil himself. I'm sure that is a gross exaggeration of how people were looking at me, but when you're on the receiving end of those looks, that is exactly how it feels.

I'm not the type to let people scare me away, most of the time, but I definitely had felt earlier that perhaps I should just crawl back under my rock. I decided to take my cue from Chuck and list all those who thought I was guilty under the heading of jesters and fools in my mind.

When the accumulated fatigue finally hit me, I suddenly realized that I had been up for most of the past 36 hours, with just a couple of cat naps to tide me over. Larry gave me a ride back to my house.

Riding in Larry's beat up '98 Ford Escort is always a bit unnerving. It might have been a nice royal blue once upon a time but now the paint was dull and there was almost more gray putty on the body than paint anyway. It had a bad habit of overheating and the brakes left a lot to be desired, but he loved that car. It had been the first and only one he had ever bought with his own money and he had had it since high school. All I knew was that it felt like I was taking my life in my hands every time I got in the thing. The car clattered up to the curb just in time for us to see Alex coming back down the sidewalk from my front door. She waived when she saw me getting out of Larry's jalopy and swerved towards us.

I said "Thanks for the ride" to Larry and, shuddering in relief to have survived, walked over to Alex.

"Y'know, you really should lock your door when you leave the house. I was headed to the store and stopped by to see if you needed anything while I was there. I saw your car in the drive but there was no answer at the door so I got worried and went inside. I realize now that you weren't home, but it gave me a scare for a couple of minutes."

"Alex, this is a really small town. Most of us still forget about locking doors and a few of the older houses probably don't even have locks on them at all. Face it, this isn't the big city, and nobody is going to break in to your house in this town. I often leave the door unlocked when I'm on a fire call; I just forget to slow down long enough to do anything about it."

"Maybe bad things never happened here in the past, but you can't really have forgotten that there is a murderer around here someplace, can you? A murderer that might welcome the chance to plant evidence to help the cops build a case against you? Keep that in mind Mister, the next time you rush out the door."

I was shocked to realize that she was right. It was just incredible to think that somebody in this small town, perhaps somebody I had known all my life, was capable of murder. Not just capable of it but had actually gone through with it. I think that's the scary part. Everybody thinks it inside their head on occasion, but it isn't something real, it isn't something that you actually do. The idea that somebody that unstable could be anyone you know, perhaps even someone living on your street, is the stuff of nightmares.

"Point taken. I have a feeling I'm going to be a lot

more careful about a lot of things in the future. I appreciate you looking after me, but I'm okay. More than anything else at this point, I think I need about eight solid hours of sleep. I'll see you later."

On the way through the living room, I checked the answering machine on my phone; there were four messages on it, one from my boss trying to apologize for this morning's scene at work, and three from some reporter down at the local paper who wanted an interview.

Shaking my head in disgust, I deleted them all and headed to the kitchen to get a beer hoping that it would help me finally get to sleep. While I was there, I also grabbed a spray bottle of cleaner and some paper towels and used them to clean the mess I had made on the wall earlier in the day when I had thrown the beer in frustration.

Eventually I headed upstairs, stripping off my running gear as I went, and climbing into bed. As tired as I was, I still tossed and turned for a while, sleep refusing to come as my mind ran in circles screaming. Eventually, I got up and took a couple of aspirin, washing them down with a fresh beer and, and stared at the TV for a while. I finally ended up falling asleep on the sofa, waking up the next morning with a sore back and a kink in my neck.

NINE

When he got back to the station Sam found the list of names and dates that Carla had left for him. Picking up the sheets he rifled through them, noticing that she appeared to have tried to be exceedingly thorough. The list of names was so long that it didn't narrow the pool of suspects very much; their house seemed to have been almost as busy as Grand Central Station over the last couple of weeks. However, he did notice that James Whitmore had been there at least twice between the times that Gus received his insulin from the VA and the day of the murder. He didn't seem to have stayed long either time, but on one of the occasions had been out in the garage area while talking to Gus. One more point in time when he was near to Gus' bottles of insulin, although there was no way to be certain if he had been left alone in the garage at any point.

Taking the list with him to his office, he plunked himself down behind the ancient grey metal desk and began to study it in detail.

Hours later, Gus slapped the file folder he'd been staring at closed and tossed it onto his desk with a disgusted groan. One hand reached up to rub tiredly at the back of his neck, aching with the tension of being bent over the desk for hours.

With a frustrated sigh, he leaned back in his chair and gazed at the office. Two months earlier, when he arrived in town, it had been a storage room filled with broken furniture and ancient crusty file cabinets. The file cabinets were still there, a row of silent watchers along the wall behind him. The walls which had been painted a blinding white when the clutter was removed were still starkly bare. The only sign that the room was in use, besides his weary form in the chair was the stacked paperwork and folders heaped randomly on the surface of the great metal desk. The air of disuse was reinforced by several sealed cardboard boxes resting against one back corner.

He could see through the window that it was completely

dark outside and realized just how long he had been staring at the list of names.

It occurred to him that the one person who had the most opportunity to tamper with the Chief's medication was the name not on the list, Mrs. Barnes herself. It made sense in a way.

Obviously, the marriage hadn't always been as solid as it appeared, or she wouldn't have had an affair with James Whitmore in the first place. Certainly living right there in the house she had all the opportunity in the world to corrupt her husband's insulin. Maybe their picture-perfect marriage was a front. On the other hand, maybe she wanted to get rid of her husband to collect the insurance and had been counting on his history of diabetes to cover up any shenanigans on her own part.

Earlier he had been thinking that perhaps Whitmore had tried to get rid of his competition in order to be with Mrs. Barnes, but perhaps, just perhaps, Mrs. Barnes had tried to get rid of an inconvenient husband to be with Whitmore. She wouldn't have been the first woman to decide the murder was easier than divorce.

The only problem was that once again, all he had was speculation. Both Mrs. Barnes and Mr. Whitmore had means, motive, and opportunity, but he didn't have a shred of evidence that pointed to either one of them. If he tried to take either one of them to court even a marginally competent lawyer would be able to point to the opposite one and make a case for reasonable doubt. God knows Alexandra Kincaid was considerably more than just competent and what she would do to him in the courtroom under these circumstances didn't even bear thinking about.

Lots of people apparently had opportunity, quite a few of those had access to the means, and that group included pretty much every member of the Fire Department. As far as he could tell only the wife and the Deputy Chief had seemed to have motive as well. In the absence of any solid evidence, they were really his only suspects.

On the way out of the office, Sam stopped in at the Administrative Department and left the folder with Carla Barnes' list of names on Suzanne Parker's desk with a quickly scrawled note requesting that she perform preliminary background checks on everyone on the list. Basically just a screen to determine if any of them had criminal records that he was unaware of. If he got unbelievably lucky, something would pop up to and point its virtual finger at someone. At the very least, he might be able to winnow down the list to something manageable.

Deciding that there was nothing else productive that he could probably get accomplished before dawn, he headed home to get a few hours well-deserved rest.

Arriving at the office early the next morning, he was flagged down by Suzanne the moment he walked through the front door.

Suzanne waved the list at him after glancing over it with a practiced eye and looked up at Sam in amazement.

"You do realize that most of these folks have lived in Element all of their lives, don't you? You really want me to go poking around in the personal lives of all these people?"

"What I want Suzanne, is to know if any of these people have any kind of criminal background or has a negative history with Chief Barnes. Can you do that or not?"

Suzanne grimaced but seeing the determined look on the detective's face, she quickly agreed to conduct the screening that he wanted. Deep down inside she hoped that nothing really big showed up on anyone. Some things about your neighbors you just didn't really ever want to know. After just that first quick glance, she was reasonably certain that nobody on that list had anything worse than a moving violation or a citation for hunting without a license. When you worked in a small town police station for more than 20 years, you already knew most of the dirt on everybody in town. After all, the entire police force for the town of Element was made up of the Chief and four deputies. At least that had been true until the chief had added Sam two months earlier.

Since Suzanne was the entire administrative department for the police force, all tickets, warrants, etc. were processed though her office. Anything nefarious that anybody did would either have to be really old news or have occurred someplace else. On the other hand, not everybody in town had lived there since birth and even those who had occasionally left town for various reasons; military service, visiting relatives, college, and the like had taken a lot of folks out of town from time to time. A computer search for any tickets, outstanding warrants, or arrests in other jurisdictions would certainly be reasonable; especially in a murder investigation.

Sighing, she added the handwritten list to the top of one of the less unstable piles on her desk and turned to the computer to access the internet. This part of the job was so much easier than it had been when she had been a rookie. The ability to log into various law enforcement data systems, as well as public records, via the internet to look up both criminal history and other records was probably the most important tool to come along in the legal field in the past 100 years.

She seriously doubted that most Americans realized that for about twelve dollars a month anybody who wanted could run a complete financial and legal background on anybody else. Everything from credit scores to driving record was available with just a few clicks of the mouse. Logging into the first site she started working her way down the list and thinking to herself that it was a shame schools don't really stress penmanship anymore. Some of the names were so illegible that if she hadn't known almost everyone in town, she never could have puzzled them out. As she worked, she kept handwritten notes about each person on a separate sheet of paper.

The whole time she was running the inquiries, which was mostly a matter of typing in a name, town, and zip code then waiting for the results to come up on the screen, she mused about detective Sam Gunne. When the Police Chief had first hired Sam as a full time detective, almost everyone thought that he had finally lost his marbles. After all, Element is a very peaceful little backwater town, at least it had been until now anyway. What was there to keep a detective busy here? The crime stats for the town were way below the national average and there hadn't been a violent crime of any kind in several years.

Of course there was the occasional assault case but it always turned out to be a couple of teenage boys in after school fights, pointing fingers each other over who threw the first punch. Certainly there hadn't been a murder in the town is long she had lived there. She had lived there since the day she was born, 38 years ago.

Most folks just decided that the Chief had a soft spot for the detective and wanted to help him out. It was common knowledge that he had been pretty burnt out when he left Kansas City. Some folks (and Suzanne happened to be one of them) thought that the Chief was betting on Sam mellowing out enough to take over as Element's top cop so that the Chief could finally retire in a couple of years. Of course, in hindsight it was probably a really good thing that he had decided to hire Sam.

It took most of the afternoon but finally she had processed every name on Carla Barnes'

list. Pushing back her chair, and wishing the department could afford one of those nice new ergonomic chairs to save her back, she stuffed the original list and all of her notes into an envelope and headed down the hall to the Spartan little room in the back that Sam called his office. Unfortunately, he wasn't there when she walked in.

Looking around the little space, she realized that there was very little to show who occupied the office, not even a name plate on the desk. Just untidy piles of paper on the desk. No pictures or award plaques like so many folks like to put in their offices. It was almost like he was afraid to do anything permanent to mark the space as his own.

Hoping that he would be able to decipher her handwriting without too much trouble, she left the envelope prominently on his chair, there being no empty space on his desk. Not that there was much of any apparent significance in what she had been able to find but there had been some rather interesting backgrounds on a couple of folks. Nothing criminal, just unexpected. With a last glance around the office, she head home early, feeling a serious headache starting to build up behind her eyes.

Her attempt to make sure that the Detective would see the results of the background checks in a timely manner would have worked a lot better if it hadn't been for the fact that the department had hired somebody to clean the ventilation ducts. As it was, the cleaning crew moved the chair, which was sitting directly below the air vent, in order to set up a stepladder to reach the vent with the vacuum and brush. When they moved it back into place, they didn't notice the envelope that had fallen on the floor near the ubiquitous grey metal filing cabinets. A few hours later, the housekeeper picked it up and set it on top of the file cabinet while emptying trash cans in the various offices.

When Sam stopped back by his desk and didn't find any messages from Suzanne, he assumed that she hadn't finished. When she wasn't at her desk, he looked up at the wall clock and decided that she must have gone home for the day and resolved to ask her for a progress report in the morning.

It was unfortunate that she never did come into work the next day, which was a Friday. In the end he didn't actually get to see the results until the following Monday since her headache had turned into a migraine. She had shut off the ringer on the phone because the sound made her skull feel as if it was going to explode.

TEN

Carla got up Sunday morning determined to talk to James, even if his lawyer didn't like it very much. She was a little surprised that he hadn't returned her call from the previous day but chalked it up to the fact that he was probably pretty distracted by all the legal complications that had come his way in the past couple days.

After brewing coffee and having some toast, she picked up the phone and dialed his home number. It was a shock when Alex Kincaid answered the phone but the other woman explained that she was meeting James that morning to discuss the case and review the available information. She had arrived just as he had returned from his morning run and so had been having coffee while he took his shower. Reassured, Carla said she just wanted to see if anything new had been learned and let him know that at least one person in town still supported him. Alex, of course, couldn't really share anything with her due to lawyer client confidentiality rules. She did promise to tell James she had called and ask him to call her back.

James:

I got up bright and early on Sunday morning, threw on some running clothes, and headed out to work off some frustration. When I got home about a half hour later, I saw Alex out in her front yard and jogged over to invite her to join me for breakfast at my place. "I'll start some coffee and go take a shower, come on over whenever you're ready."

I finished my shower and was shaving when I heard the phone ring downstairs, quickly followed by somebody talking. I finished up, headed downstairs still toweling my hair dry, and checked the call log on my phone, noting that it had been Carla Barnes that had called. I headed to the kitchen only to find Alex in the kitchen, sipping on a mug of coffee, "I poured you a cup of coffee but I wasn't sure how you like it. So right now, it's just black. Good coffee though."

"Black is just fine thanks. Who was that on the phone

just now?"

Alex looked a bit sheepish about having answered my phone, but didn't hesitate to answer my question, "Carla Barnes called. She said she had heard that the police cleared you of Gus' murder, and she wanted to know if it was true. She sounded a bit surprised, which I thought was a bit odd. Oh well, she's probably just still stunned about the police, claiming Gus was murdered. After all, for the first several days his death had been classed as accidental."

I opened the refrigerator and pulled out a carton of eggs and some nice sharp cheddar cheese. As I continued to rummage about for the bell peppers, onions and margarine, I glanced up at Alex in wonder. From her tone and the sort of exaggerated casual way that she had dropped that comment about Carla, It almost seemed that she was trying to imply that Carla might have known that Gus' death wasn't accidental all along. Somehow, I just couldn't bring myself to even think such a thing about a woman that I had been so close to, one that I knew in my heart had been truly dedicated to her husband. "Are you trying to imply something counselor? ,,Cause if you are, I'm not buying it. Carla Barnes didn't know about Gus' murder before the police told us. I'll bet my life on it."

She looked over at me with what appeared to be real surprise at my tone.

"James, I'm sorry. I only meant that it must have been a shock to find out that her husband was murdered. Why don't we get off this macabre subject and onto breakfast? What are you feeding me anyway?'

She seemed sincere enough. Maybe she was just a tiny bit jealous of my past relationship with Carla, and it was coming out as a touch of cattiness. I could hope so anyway.

"A western omelet, I think, I can't seem to find the picante' sauce". I turned back to the fridge to continue my search but heard her from right behind me, "Don't worry about it, the omelet will be just fine without it".

I turned around to find her just inches away from me. With the high heels she was wearing, we were basically eye-to-eye. At that range, her perfume was rather intoxicating, as if the woman herself wasn't overpowering enough to my rather deprived male senses. It had been a long time since I had been this close to a female that wasn't covered in blood, or hives, or in some other totally un-sexy situation. I found myself unexpectedly nervous so of course I botched things altogether...edging past her to reach a cabinet next to the microwave.

"No problem, I'm pretty sure that I have a fresh bottle in here."

I turned around and was treated to the sight of her practically slinking across the kitchen in my direction. I just stood there feeling like a mouse being stalked by a Siamese cat. I swear I could almost hear her purring. She stopped when we were toe to toe and put her hands on my chest, curling her nails into the flesh slightly before murmuring huskily in me ear.

"Actually, I'm really not all that hungry at the moment, for eggs."

I put my hands up and took hold of her wrists, hardly believing the next words out of my own mouth.

"Look Alex, I think you're moving a bit too quick for me. Not that I haven't thought of this more than a few times, but is this really a good idea when you're my lawyer and this whole murder investigation is still unresolved?"

Part of my brain knew it was the right

thing to say and the other part was calling me seventeen kinds of idiot for turning her down, especially when I had been thinking about this while coming down stairs; thoughts I had been having a great deal the last couple of days. She smiled at me and stepped back, a single step.

"You're right, it probably isn't wise. Do you always to the wise thing James? Don't you ever just throw caution to the winds?"

"Not often, at least not in a long time."

She stepped back a bit further and looked at me closer. After a long moment, she appeared to make a decision and nodded slightly. Turning on her heel, she left the kitchen, walking towards the front of the house. I stood there stunned for a second and then took off after her. I came around the corner and found her sitting on the sofa in the living room, waiting for me. I walked over and sat next to her, only to be surprised once again when she asked me about Sara.

"Look James, why don't we start over and get to know each other a little better? I know it sounds a bit like a cliché' but it makes sense to slow down, especially because you're absolutely right, I'm your lawyer and for now that means that we really shouldn't cross that line. I apologize for creating an awkward situation."

Before I knew it, I was telling her about Sara and the divorce. About Sara's fears and my inability to walk away from the station, even to save my marriage or to spare the woman I loved from the misery of being afraid all the time. I told her all of the things that I had been holding inside for so long. I was kind of ashamed of my selfishness and what it had done to Sara; something that nobody but Carla had ever really understood before. Alex seemed to figure it out and just sort of pulled it out of me. It made me wonder about lawyers. Just how much their work could be similar to psychoanalysis. Both professions involve figuring out peoples motives and finding those truths that people try to hide, even from themselves. She was awfully good at it and I found it amazing that I was pouring all this baggage out on a woman that I wanted so desperately to impress.

We talked for hours and by dinner time, I'm not sure that there was much we didn't know about each other. At least not much that she didn't know about me. I spent a lot of time telling her about Sara. My beautiful Sara, who had been my high school sweetheart and best friend for years before that, we had in fact been friends since grade school; a real fairytale story. Only we hadn't managed to live happily ever after. When I first joined the department at 16, she thought it was dashing and romantic. She loved the idea of me as sort of a modern day knight, out rescuing damsels in distress. I have to admit, all of that wide-eyed, breathless awe she was sending my way had been pretty heady stuff for a sort of shy teenage boy. To have the most stunningly beautiful girl in town as both my best friend and returning my romantic interest would have been enough to overwhelm any guy at that age. I had eaten it up.

High school sweethearts, then I went away for a hitch in the Navy. We spent a fortune on letters and phone calls, the whole time I was gone, but I wouldn't have changed it given the chance. It was the Navy that taught me electronics and telecommunications, skills I had built into a successful career in installing and maintaining the 911 communications system for the county. Of course, I spent almost as much time on the road as I did at the home office, but it was work I enjoyed. Being the only person covering about 900 miles, it usually afforded the chance to pick up a fair amount of overtime.

Sara and I had gotten married while I was on leave, about halfway through my hitch in the Navy and she had stayed home because I was stationed on a ship at the time. When I got out and came back to Element, we had moved into the house my parents left me and I had rejoined the department. It wasn't long before she started to get increasingly panicked every time the pager went off. In retrospect, it probably had a lot to do with the fact that I was now actually going into the burning buildings. Cadet firefighters (under the age of 18) are not allowed to actually go into fires, so being a cadet was safe. Her fear started around the time I started fighting fires for real, so it seems a reasonable explanation.

Anyway, she managed to cope with it for a long time, but after 10 years, it finally came down to me giving up the one thing I loved doing or giving up Sara. In the end, I had come home one day and found that she was gone. I couldn't change who I was, not without losing myself altogether, and she couldn't cope with who I was. I let her go rather than make either of us even more miserable than we already were. She moved back in with her folks and filed for divorce. With no kids or pets, and me inheriting the house from my parents, there really wasn't any reason to fight over who got what, so it was all very civil. We split the bills 50-50, and I agreed to pay alimony for three years while she saved for a place of her own, and finished college. A year later, she had died in my arms, a casualty of my adherence to department protocols.

Alex sat there and quietly listened to me ramble. When I finally wound down to silence,

we just sat there, her holding my hand, for a really long time. Finally, she looked at me and said,

"How long has it been since you took some time off and got out of town? You know did something just for fun?"

I must've looked confused because she sat back and gave a light laugh.

"I thought so. I have a small cabin about a mile west of Miller's Creek. How about when this is all over we go up there for the weekend just you me and the squirrels."

I chuckled, "I thought you wanted to be alone with me? Why invite the whole station?"

I knew what she meant but I couldn't resist the urge to tease her over her unintended pun. Of course, I then had to explain those volunteer firefighters who were really into it, the ones who live and breathe it spending every waking moment at the station, were called squirrels by a lot of people. At least were referred to as being a bit squirrelly. It was a good gambit, the mood had gotten way too somber, and the moment of humor helped bring things back into focus. As for her idea about a trip up to her cabin, I once again had the interest of the most beautiful woman in town and I wasn't about to say no.

Having spent most of the afternoon sitting on my sofa talking, we decided to get some dinner. As we were leaving, and I was turning to lock the house; I heard Alex from behind me,

"Isn't that Flash?"

I looked up and saw the Barnes' Dalmatian, Flash, wandering down the street. Gus had thought the idea of the Fire Chief having a Dalmatian dog was just hysterically funny. Even though Carla was more of a cat person, she had gotten Flash for Gus as a birthday present, about six or seven years ago. The dog was wondering down the sidewalk checking out every tree and car as he went. When I whistled sharply and called his name, he came galloping over to us. Carla had once made the comment that a Dalmatian was just a Greyhound with a polka dot paint job. Watching him racing towards us across the lawn, I could believe it. He barreled up the front steps and launched himself at me. Then he threw himself at Alex, barking and licking her face in ecstasy. I looked at her in surprise.

"Wow, do you two know each other? He doesn't usually take to strangers that fast."

Alex ruffled his ears and made good doggie noises at him, while laughing at me. It seems that her and Flash were old friends. A couple of month's back she had been his dog sitter for several days; when Gus and Carla had gone up to Jackson Hole Wyoming for his sister's wedding.

Alex and I loaded Flash in my car and headed for the Barnes' house to take him home. When we rang the bell, Carla appeared with a phone held to her ear. She was in the middle of telling someone that Flash had run off again when she opened the door and discovered the three of us standing on her front porch.

"Never mind, James and Alex just brought him home. Thanks anyway. Yeah, I'll call you tomorrow." Hanging up the phone, she turned her attention to the three of us standing outside her front door.

"Oh thank goodness! I'm glad you found him. The stupid animal ran off again this morning and I was just starting to call people to find out if they've seen him. Where did you catch up with him?"

"He was headed down our street and we saw him as we were headed out to get something to eat." I glanced over at Alex and back to Carla, "I was surprised when he ran up and jumped all over Alex. I didn't know the big lug knew her."

"Alex dog sat for us a couple months ago when Gus and I went over to Jackson Hole for his sister's wedding. I guess they got along pretty well."

Carla smiled at us and appeared to be pleased that I finally appeared to be developing a social life. It least it must have looked that way to her from the way Alex and I were standing so close together. It was nice to see her smiling.

"I just want you to know James; I don't believe for a moment that you could've ever had anything to do with hurting Gus. I think the whole idea is just crazy, and I said so to the detective when he was talking to me about the case."

I smiled fondly at her, "Thanks Carla that means a lot to me. It really is hard to have people turning away because they think you're some kind of murderous monster. It's good to know that I still have a few friends. I appreciate your support."

What followed was a slightly awkward moment of silence while Carla seemed to wonder if she ought to invite us in and we wondered how to end the conversation and leave so we could get some dinner. Finally, Alex suggested that we really had to get going, as she said it she slipped her hand through my arm to hold on to my elbow. She stepped in even closer and smiled at Carla with what looked to me like just a hint of possession. Carla acknowledged her with a tiny nod and a smile in return,

"Of course. You mustn't let me keep you from your dinner. I really appreciate the two of you returning Flash".

--

Having spent a rather startling amount of the day talking about myself, over dinner, I tried to get Alex to tell me more about her. Up to that point all I really knew was that she was a lawyer and had grown up in Kansas City. She had moved to Element when she decided to ditch the big city in favor of the tranquility of small-town living. After initially trying to get out of talking by claiming not to be very interesting (something I didn't believe for a moment), she did open up a bit. She had indeed grown up in Kansas City. She put herself through college and law school on a combination of scholarships, grants, and student loans and had been a partner in a successful law practice before deciding to move to our little back corner of the world.

Somehow, that seems like a rather skimpy personal history after all of the heavy stuff I had unloaded that afternoon. I was really interested, she seemed to have accomplished a great deal along the way and was trying to gloss it over. I wasn't about to let her get away with it. I guess I can get a bit pushy when I really want to and that evening I really wanted to. I kept throwing questions at her; did she have any siblings, what were her parents like, what part Kansas City had she lived in, and did she have any pets? She finally gave in and started to tell me more; probably out of sheer exasperation. What came out was a very different story than I had been expecting and after hearing it, it was a lot easier to understand why she was reluctant to talk about her youth.

Alex had grown up in the worst part of the city. She had never known her father and her mother had been a serious basket case; having gotten hooked on both drugs and alcohol shortly after Alex was born. In other words, she had pretty much grown up in foster care. I know enough to understand that there is a good foster care and bad foster care; her experience had gone well beyond merely bad. There had been a series of foster homes where she had been nothing more than an additional burden and an extra check from the city. Yes, there had been some decent homes along the way but she never seemed to get to stay in them. The other homes she really wanted nothing more than to forget. She didn't tell me everything but she told me enough for me to understand that some of it had been really, really bad.

In a monumental effort and by sheer stubborn determination, she had managed to hang on long enough to graduate high school, but she had been out the door the same day that she got her diploma. More than anything else, she had promised herself that she would get out of the slums she had grown up in and that nothing would ever cause her to go back. She worked like a demon to make it through college and law school on her own. In the end, she succeeded admirably, but she still carried an obsession to give herself the independence and the financial stability that she had lacked as a child. To never again live in hunger or fear. She was, without a doubt, the strongest person I've ever known in my entire life.

Over the years, she had spent a considerable amount of energy trying to track down her father. It wasn't easy because her mother, on those rare occasions when she had actually seen her, would never say who he was. Her birth certificate hadn't given his name either, listing him as "father unknown". It wasn't something she really believed based on occasional hints that she had gleaned from her mother and later on from her mother's personal effects. Apparently, after her mother had died, Alex had combed through what little she had owned in an effort to find clues to her father's identity. There hadn't been much. When I asked her if she was still searching for him she had replied,

"No, I'm not looking for him anymore. I've moved beyond that."

I can remember thinking how incredibly sad that was and I resolved to help her regain her enthusiasm for the hunt.

Perhaps even help her track down her father and settle some of the questions she must have had.

ELEVEN

Sam was at his desk Sunday when Alexandra Kincaid walked into his office. He was off on the weekends, but in realistic terms, he wasn't going to get much sleep until he solved this case. He would take time off when somebody was behind bars for the murder of Gus Barnes. He watched her striding purposefully across the foyer towards him, admiring the panther-like grace of her movements. No wasted energy, just purpose and fluid movement.

Giving him a predatory look, she went immediately on the offensive as she settled herself into the chair across from him, crossing her legs and treating him to a scintillating view of long tanned shapely legs.

"Any progress on the Barnes case detective? Please keep in mind my client's job takes him out of town and across half the state at times. He needs to be able to move around."

"Nothing relevant counselor. I'm still waiting for background information on a number of people connected with the Chief. I've nothing substantial on which to hold your client at this int. I if I did he wouldn't be walking around free."

"I'm sure he'll be glad to hear it," she purred. "By the way, were you aware that the fire department maintains life insurance policies on its members? If they die in the station or on an emergency call, the policy pays out a million dollars."

She paused for effect, "I give you one guess who gets the money from the policy on Chief Barnes."

He gave her a tired look that clearly showed his annoyance with civilians that tried to do his job for him.

"Probably his wife Carla. Why?"

"Are you kidding detective? It seems to me that a million dollars is pretty substantial motive for murder. When you consider that it was also staged to look like a natural death, it makes even more sense. Most insurance policies have clauses to prevent payment if the deceased is murdered, especially if the murderer is the beneficiary. So if Carla murdered her husband, and I'm not saying she did, it would be imperative for her to make it look like natural causes."

Sam looked thoughtfully at her before conceding the point. He had known about the normal life insurance policy on Gus but it had only been for about $100,000, enough to pay off bills and provide a small annuity. Certainly not enough to normally push someone to murder. Then again, people have committed murder for whole lot less.

"So what you're really doing is being gracious enough to provide me with another suspect, moving the focus off of your client. Is that about right counselor?"

Of course, that made perfect sense since her job as his lawyer was to do whatever was best for him, without regard for other people.

They continued to talk for a couple of minutes before she left after which he went over to talk to the admin secretary for the volunteer fire organization, Wendy Wallace. A very short conversation with her confirmed that the organization did in fact carry a large policy designed to provide for the families of members who fell in the line of duty and death at the station was certainly qualifying. Carla Barnes would be the recipient in the case of Chief Barnes. Then she also confirmed for him that the payout on the life insurance was being held up by the insurance company until the identity of the person who had killed Chief Barnes was resolved. They wouldn't chance paying out to any individual who might have been involved in his death.

Deciding that staring at the mess on his desk all afternoon wasn't going to do any good, he decided to pack it in and try to relax for the remainder of the day. Perhaps if he took his mind off the case for a bit it would help him salvage some perspective on the information.

Sam stopped in the office Monday morning. After a quick check of his voice messages (there weren't any), he set out in search of Suzanne and the background checks he had asked for. She was apparently finally over whatever it was that had laid her low the previous week and was at her desk looking annoyingly chipper for first thing on a Monday morning. Sam, on the other hand was out of sorts with the entire universe. He hadn't slept well all weekend because his mind kept coming back to the case and his frustration at not having solved it already. He knew from experience that the longer a case lingers, the more likely it would go unsolved forever. In a town this size, he ought to be able to find a single cold blooded killer. He was well aware that most folks had thought it was foolish to have hired a full time detective in this quiet corner of South Dakota. If he couldn't wrap this case up soon he would only prove their point. It wouldn't do much for his shaky self-confidence either. As a result, he all but snarled at a very startled Suzanne in the course of asking about the background checks.

When Sam showed up in her office, Suzanne was trying her best to be pleasant, a hard task early on a Monday. She really kind of liked him and wanted to make a good impression. That was part of the reason she had stayed until she was done collecting the information he had requested before leaving last week; even though she really hadn't been feeling well.

When he stomped in and practically chewed her head off for not getting the information to him, it was all she could do not to burst into tears right then and there. Well, it was either break down and cry or go on the attack. Her own eyes narrowed as she stared angrily back at him.

"What are you talking about? I put those results on your desk before I left on Thursday. I placed them in an envelope right on your chair and wrote your name on the front of the envelope. So don't come in here yelling at me that I didn't do my job. Try looking around in that mess you call an office instead of accusing me when I know full well that those results were right there for you, just as you asked."

Sam took a step back surprised by the vehemence of her response. Up until now, Suzanne had been a bit on the meek side and he had never heard her raise her voice at anyone before. Right now she was almost giving off sparks she was so mad at him. While he didn't generally like having women angry with him, he thought to himself that it did give a certain sparkle to her eyes. He decided he'd better take a different tack or she would never talk to him again.

"Look Suzanne I'm sorry. I didn't mean to come in here and tear into you like that. I've been in my office. I was in the office a good deal over the weekend and I never saw the envelope you're talking about. I just assumed that you hadn't finished it because you weren't feeling well on Friday. I know that's no excuse for me being a complete idiot about it this morning but it's been a very long and frustrating weekend and I'm about at my wits end trying to figure out this case. Do you have any thoughts on what might've happened to it after you put it on my desk? Is it possible somebody else took it?"

Deciding to take pity on him since he apparently hadn't had any coffee yet that morning, Suzanne rose from behind her desk and came around towards him. As she did, she noticed that he was only a couple of inches taller than she was, so they were nearly eye to eye. It was a pleasant change from the six foot four, high school football player deputies that tended to be the standard in the department. He really wasn't bad looking either, just kind of tired looking all the time; like he had seen too much and it didn't let him sleep well.

"Look detective, it seems we both started off on the wrong foot this morning. Why don't we go back to your office together and take a look around. Maybe we can figure out what happened to the envelope. If we can't find it I'll redo them before lunch, but let's make sure first that they're really gone. Okay?"

She smiled tentatively at him and waved towards the office door in sort of a general, 'shall we go' type motion. When he nodded in return, she pivoted around and headed towards his office.

The two of them proceeded to sort through all the random bits of paper and folders sitting on his desk but there was no sign of the envelope. Suzanne started to look around at the stuff on top of everything else. There were files and papers stacked on top of the filing cabinets, which she suspected were mostly empty. Really, she thought as she moved around the room, what this man needs most is a maid for his office. I don't know why he has three filling cabinets when it seems like everything is piled on top of them and the desk instead of inside them. She had to wonder how a man who had only worked there for two months and really hadn't had any major cases to solve could've accumulated so much paperwork. It seemed like almost as much of a mystery as the murder.

At any rate, she started at one side of the filing cabinets, sorting through the paperwork on top of the right-hand cabinet in a methodical way that ensured nothing would be missed. When she moved to the center cabinet the manila envelope that she'd put on his chair was sitting right on top of it.

Picking it up, she turned towards him with a satisfied grin and waved the envelope in front of his face.

"I knew I put it in your office. You must've picked it up with some other papers and stacked it up here without paying any attention to what might be in it. Do you have anything to say now detective?"

"Only that I know is that I didn't put it up there. I don't remember putting anything on that filing cabinet on Friday. However, it's there and I owe you an apology. I should've realized that at the very least you would've left me a note if you truly hadn't finished them. All I can say is it's a Monday morning, I haven't had any coffee, and very little sleep and I've been acting like a fool. Am I forgiven?"

He tried giving her a woebegone puppy dog look, but it really didn't work very well on his face. It did however make Suzanne laugh and that was worth something.

"Oh I give up. One of these days, we're going to have to do something about this office. I don't know how you can find your car keys much less important evidence in here. In the meantime, by way of apology you can buy me a cup of coffee."

Sam figured he was getting off easy all things considered and quickly agreed but asked for rain check because he really wanted to dive into the results of the background checks she had done.

Looking at him again, she came to an instant decision that he probably needed more than coffee, he probably hadn't been eating right either.

"Bachelors", she muttered in exasperation under her breath.

"Why don't we go over to the Lazy Dog and grab some breakfast. We can go over the list together while we eat. Honestly though, I don't think you'll find what you're looking for in there. There really wasn't much beyond a few moving violations and youthful indiscretions. Nobody in town seems to be harboring any major criminal activities in their past. No deep dark secrets or malevolent obsessions. Just ordinary people living ordinary lives. None of it makes any sense. All I can say is somebody sure must've been mad at Gus; but whoever it was must sure have been hiding it well."

Her words really didn't make him feel any better. It was nice that she accepted his apology, but if there really wasn't anything, useful in the information she had gathered then he was right back at square one. He hesitated, wanting to take immediate action of some kind after losing most of the weekend but eventually realized that she was right; sitting at his desk, going over the same evidence again and again wasn't getting him anywhere.

Perhaps a fresh perspective was exactly what he needed. A second brain to filter the information might be really helpful and breakfast seemed like a reasonable apology for his rude behavior. He nodded his head and gestured towards the door as if to say, 'after you'.

The Lazy Dog was the only diner in town and at 9AM on a Monday morning, the only other customers were an elderly couple enjoying their meal at a table near the front window. They settled into a booth at the back where a crisp red-and-white checked tablecloth covered the battered Formica table and where Sam felt they could discuss the case without being overheard.

Over coffee, eggs, and bacon, Suzanne ran down the list of minor offenses and other relatively trivial information that she had uncovered. Wendell Carver, deacon at the Baptist Church and 15 year member of the Fire Department, apparently had owned a pawn shop in Billings, Montana years ago. The shop had closed when the police started wondering about the legality of some merchandise (but he had never been charged with anything illegal). That was it, the deepest, darkest, most horrible thing she had found in the background of anybody on the list. Otherwise it was all traffic tickets and such; certainly nothing violent among the group.

Sam sat back and rested his head against the high wooden back of the booth wall, closing his eyes in dismay. When he finally opened them again, Suzanne was studying him intently.

"What are you thinking?"

"I was running over the possible motives for murder. Since nobody else seems to have had any reason to want Gus dead, I keep coming back to either his wife or Whitmore as suspects." She considered this for a moment. "Maybe I'm just not looking for the right things. After all, I've never had to do research trying to find a motive for murder. What I know about it mostly comes from watching TV."

He winced a bit at that thought and she grinned.

"Not much of a resume for helping out, is it?"

He shrugged slightly and then proceeded to run down his personal top motives list for her. "The most common reasons for killing someone are generally vengeance, money, power, or sex. Nobody seems to have had vengeance as a motive except James Whitmore. It's possible that somebody else used a random opportunity to get even with him for something but we haven't found any evidence of anybody with a grudge except Whitmore for the public argument and losing the station election. Although that was my first impression immediately after the coroner has classed the case as a homicide, now it seems like a bit of a stretch, vengeance is usually a long-term motive and this seemed too well thought out for someone grabbing at a chance opportunity."

It couldn't be discounted altogether, but it wasn't the top of the motive list unless somebody else with a grudge turned up. That left money, sex, and power as possible motives in this case.

"Well, if we eliminate vengeance as the motive; what about sex, power, or money? I know that Carla had an affair with James a while back that ended amicably. At least they all seem to be friends. I don't see that as being a reason for her to kill him, do you?"

"Not really. Although I suppose that if James and Carla wanted to rekindle their affair that they might want to get rid of Gus to avoid complications. But it really seems like that would create more complications than it avoided. What about Gus? Have you ever heard any rumors of him having an affair?"

She paused to think back, biting her bottom lip in concentration.

"Not that I remember. Of course, I can't swear that I've heard about every affair that happened in this town. But he just doesn't seem the type to cheat on his wife."

She watched as Sam stirred his eggs again without so much as tasting them. The eggs, originally sunny side up, were now thoroughly scrambled. In a moment of clarity, she recalled something she had read while transcribing interviews with witnesses from the station.

"Wait a minute, wasn't there something mentioned by one of the people at the business meeting about Gus giving "special" training one of the female members?"

Sam looked up from his now scrambled eggs in surprise.

"In the interview reports?"

"Yeah, I seem to recall something like that. But everybody seemed to discount it as just sour grapes on Whitmore's part. I'm pretty certain that it was Whitmore who said it."

She tipped her head to the side slightly as she thought and then took a long sip of the now tepid coffee sitting on the table in front of her before continuing.

"Well, if we eliminate vengeance and sex I suppose that leaves money and power. The power part seems kind of obvious, the only one that I can think of that stands to gain power of any kind by the chiefs death is the deputy chief. He gets an instant promotion. Doesn't seem like much of a motive for killing somebody though. You know what I mean?"

"I know exactly what you mean. But one thing I've learned over the years is that murderer can be motivated by the strangest things, things in significant enough that nobody else but the murderer really cares about them. I've known people to be murdered for far less than that. Hell, in Kansas City we had teenagers killing each other for a pair of sneakers or designer jeans. If people are willing to kill each other over a pair of shoes then why not to gain a position of power, authority, and respect?"

She looked up at the ceiling squinting slightly as if she was trying to focus her thoughts. She took another long swig of her coffee, shuddered slightly at the taste of the cooling brew, and shrugged.

"Maybe so but I just don't see it in this case."

"Well, that only leaves money then." The only money we know about is from two insurance policies. Gus certainly wasn't wealthy but the life insurance from the station was significant enough to be enticing for murder, especially if his 401(k) at work or some other insurance policy was also large as well. His wife certainly wouldn't be the first woman to try killing her husband for the insurance."

"But why eliminate sex as a motive? It could still be the wife's motive. Both she and Whitmore admitted to the affair several years ago. She could have decided that she would rather be with James after all. Perhaps the Chief had found out and planned to make trouble. On the other hand, perhaps he had threatened to cut her off from any support if she left him; which goes back to money again doesn't it? Maybe, James decided that he wanted her back and felt that getting rid of her husband would leave her free to return to him."

"If that's the case, he's sure playing it close because there aren't any indications that they have rekindled their old romance."

"That we know of."

"Yeah. But it's certainly something to look into. If they rekindled their relationship perhaps a neighbor may have noticed something."

Sam seemed to perk up slightly at this idea and she assumed that it was because there was a new angle to check into.

"The motive could even have been a combination of money, sex, and power if you assume a conspiracy between his wife and her supposedly former lover. She would get money and sex and he would get sex and power. It makes kind of an attractive backdrop for murder."

Sam sighed. "There's only one problem with that theory and with all these theories when you get down to it. Not a shred of real evidence points to any of them."

Sam finished off his breakfast, brushing crumbs from his

shirt front, and got up from the table resolving to have another conversation with Carla Barnes as well as looking into her financial status and interviewing neighbors near both houses. Perhaps he also ought to check motels within a reasonable driving distance.

Thanking Suzanne once again for her

help, he dropped her off at the Police Station and headed off to interrogate Carla Barnes.

Twelve

Sam pulled up in front of the Barnes house and got out of his car. Before heading up to the house, he stopped and once again took a moment to look over the front side of the property. There was a small but tidy yard out front with a pretty little flower garden that ran along one side of the porch. The well maintained exterior looked like it had been painted in the not too distant past. A nice house in a nice town that belonged to nice people, in theory.

Mentally shrugging he headed up the four wide steps and across the covered porch to ring the doorbell. No answer. He waited about a minute and rang the bell again. Still no answer, not even the dog seemed to be moving about. He tested the door and found it locked so he decided to walk around the side of the house towards the backyard in case Carla was out there.

Walking across the lawn, he noted that there wasn't so much as dandelion in sight. Everything seemed to be perfectly trimmed and well maintained. Walking up the driveway towards the side gate next to the garage, he paused to glance in through the glass windows on the front of the garage door, making note of the fact that Mrs. Barnes car was in the garage. The side gate was standing open and he walked through and around in the backyard. That was when he noticed the back door standing open.

Odd, he thought, it's not normal for a person with a

dog to leave both the door and a gate standing open. Then again, the dog does have a history of running away; maybe that's how it happens. Anyway, there's only one way to find out, and that's by asking Mrs. Barnes.

He walked across the yard and over to the open back door. As he approached the door, he called out her name but was met only by silence. He was starting to get that tingle at the base of his skull that meant something was very, very wrong. At the very least, he would expect the dog to bark at someone walking into the house. He stepped to the doorway and peered inside the back entrance and through to the kitchen. The kitchen was a shambles, and even from the doorway, he could see a dark wet looking smear on the floor. There was a slightly metallic smell which left a tang in the back of his throat and called up memories of blood spattered crime scenes from the past. He stepped back and dug his cell phone out of its holster on his hip, dialing station and asking for backup.

He knew he really ought to wait for backup, but he also knew that if Mrs. Barnes was injured every moment he hesitated could be deadly. He entered the house; stepping gingerly and trying not to disturb anything. He took three steps across the back entryway to the kitchen door which gave him a full view of the kitchen area. There were dishes in the sink, and at least a couple appeared to have been broken. There were shards on both the counter and the floor. The table seemed to be off-center from where he remembered it from his previous time at the house and a couple of chairs were overturned, pushed to the side as well.

Far more important than all of that was the large black pool of blood which spread out around the body of the Barnes' Dalmatian dog. From the amount of blood and the gaping wound on the dog's neck it was obviously too late to save him. Looking at the blood, he could see that the edges of the pool were dry which meant that whatever had happened here had happened hours earlier. It also meant that he might have another murder on his hands.

He made a very quick check of all the rooms just to make sure that Carla Barnes wasn't in the house and injured before he stepped back outside to wait for backup and ask that the station once again request the services of the evidence technician from the County Sheriff's office. It really would've been best to have an evidence technician on hand, but Element was just too small a town to need both the detective and a technician on staff. There was one county technician that lived just outside of town and only worked part time, generally doing on call work. Because he lived so close to the town having him on call was almost as good as having him on staff. It only became an issue if he was needed somewhere else in the county at the same time. However, that hadn't happened yet.

While he was waiting for the others to show up Sam stood on the front sidewalk got out his notepad and opened it to a blank page to write down his impressions, thoughts, and observations regarding the current situation. As he ran through the facts in his mind he jotted them down using his own personal shorthand which when combined with his lousy chicken scratch handwriting, made his notes virtually undecipherable by anybody but him (and Suzanne he realized, somewhat startled). First thought: whatever happened here apparently happened sometime during the early morning hours; probably close to dawn, considering the pool of blood around the dog hadn't totally dried yet.

There had been a struggle that much was obvious and Carla Barnes was missing. Whoever she had been struggling with probably killed the dog to keep it quiet or to protect themselves if the dog had been trying to protect its mistress. Possibly a combination of both. Sam had a bit of a soft spot for animals and someone who would harm a dog almost upset him more than someone who would harm a person had.

The one piece that puzzled him was; why was Carla missing? If she had been attacked by the same person that killed her husband, why hadn't they simply killed her as well? Of course, if you really wanted to attribute her husband's murder to her, the evidence of a fight and the dead dog could've been staged to make it look like she had been kidnapped when really she had just left town to avoid prosecution. Anything was possible and he'd certainly seen enough sociopaths in his career to know that, but Carla Barnes just didn't seem to fit the profile.

When police cars and the evidence van all started pulling up to the curb out front of the house, the neighbors also started to come out. Sam took a few moments to brief the technician so that he could begin his job inside and to instruct the two officers to put up the crime scene tape around the property to keep everybody but the technician, Sam, and the police Chief out of the scene.

That done he decided to ask the neighbors if anybody had heard anything in the night or early morning hours. Unfortunately, everybody on the block seemed to be extraordinarily sound sleepers; nobody had seen or heard anything. The only people anybody remembered being there last night were James Whitmore and his attorney, Alexandra Kincaid, who had apparently brought the dog home early in the evening. There was James Whitmore's name popping up again in a timely, or not so timely, fashion in relation to something bad happening to somebody. At least this time there seemed to be a greater likelihood of finding some solid evidence at the scene.

He checked in quickly with the technician to find out if anything that might be useful had shown up yet and gave the man his cell phone number with instructions to call at any time if something did come up. That done, he headed over to have a little chat with James Whitmore. It just bothered him enormously that the man's name kept coming up in association with the Barnes couple and tragic events. It just felt like there had to be some kind of connection, if he could only figure out what it was.

It didn't take long to go between the two houses since it was only about 3 blocks over to Whitmore's house. As a result, he pulled up out front at around ten forty-five in the morning. Unfortunately, since it was a work day, nobody was home. As he headed back down the walk to his car, Gladys Jackson popped out of her house and headed towards him, a determined look on her face. Sam groaned inside but was careful not to show his annoyance.

Gladys Jackson was the town busybody and always had something to say about anything and anyone, no matter what the circumstances. Most of the time what she wanted to say wasn't anything more than minor gossip and malicious innuendo so talking to her could be extremely irritating.

He was steeling himself to deal with her, resolving to cut himself free as quickly as possible, when it occurred to him that she might be able to answer a couple of key questions for him. Certainly, if anything odd had happened on her street she would know…and be willing to share the information. By the time he came face to face with her, he was looking forward to the conversation with an unusual level of enthusiasm. He had barely begun to say hello when she broke in on him.

"Good morning detective, are you looking for James Whitmore? He's not home. He was out with that blonde floozy that lives next door to him last night. They got back about nine pm and both went into his house. Then he got in his car and drove off about three o'clock this morning. I haven't seen her but she might have left while I was taking my shower. Is he still a suspect in Chief Barnes' murder? I always thought he was a little too goodie-goodie if you know what I mean. There was just something I didn't quite trust about him or that Kincaid woman either for that fact. I knew that he was probably up to no good." She took a deep breath, her right hand reaching up to clutch her chest for dramatic emphasis before continuing her diatribe. "When I think that there has been a killer living right here on our street I just can't quite grasp it. Why, we might all have been murdered in our sleep! The very idea of such a person running loose in our little town terrifies me. I tell you I won't be able to sleep a wink knowing that he is out there, ready to pounce on any one of us at any moment..."

Really, the woman was a menace to everyone around her. On the other hand, she had answered his question for him with a great deal of certainty. It appeared that James Whitmore had left his house at a time that would have easily allowed him to be involved in whatever had happened to Carla Barnes. Since his car was still in the driveway, it was likely that he had taken the truck from the telephone company or walked. If he had kidnapped Carla Barnes, then it was likely that he had taken the truck. Most of the utility support staff (and cops as well for that matter) in town took the company vehicles home at night in case they were called to deal with an emergency.

He tried to stem the tide of words spewing from the woman in front of him, but it wasn't easy. Once Gladys Jackson got started, it was almost impossible to shut her down. In the end, he just let her continue until she had to pause for air. As soon as she did, he jumped in.

"Thank you for the information Gladys. I appreciate that you're trying to help the investigation. I really have to get back to the station to check out a few things."

He edged further away from her in the direction of his car.

"I ought to tell you though that you really shouldn't go around saying that anybody is a killer. There's no proof and it could be grounds for a libel suit down the road".

He turned and walked back to the car as fast as he could without appearing to be running away. He practically jumped in behind the wheel and had to concentrate on not gunning it to get out of sight as fast as possible.

When he turned the corner and was reasonably sure she couldn't see him anymore, he pulled over to the curb and shut off the engine in order to consider his next step. It appeared that James Whitmore might once again be at the top of his suspect list. On the other hand, it was likely that Carla had moved from the suspect column to the victim column overnight. The next step was see if Whitmore had a legitimate reason for leaving home at three in the morning. Mindful of his advice to Gladys Jackson, Sam didn't want to overstep and point fingers at anybody too soon, again. The Chief hadn't been very happy about his premature arrest of Whitmore the first time. Before picking him up again, he better actually have some evidence to back it up or his butt would be on the line for sure.

OK. If he took the company truck then the best place to start would be the telephone company offices. Check to see if they had dispatched him in the early morning hours. Another thing he needed to do was to ask Suzanne to expand the scope of the background checks on James Whitmore and Carla Barnes. He needed more depth on James as his primary suspect and he certainly needed more on Carla in hopes of finding some clue to tell him what had happened to her and why.

Feeling a bit better since he at least knew what to do next, Sam started the car back up and drove to the office. The first thing he did when he got there was to stop in to see Suzanne and ask her to see what else she could find by expanding the background searches on James and Carla. He was glad to see that Suzanne's mood seemed to have improved a great deal after their first rocky start that morning. From all indications, he was back in her good graces. Providing her with little more than the bare facts of Carla's disappearance, he asked her to dig as deep as she could as quickly as possible. He also gave her his cell phone number in case he was out of the office when anything relevant turned up.

Having done that, he grabbed the phone directory from the desk out front and looked up the business phone number for the telephone company. His call was answered by a pleasant sounding person with a young voice who asked how they could help him. The individual on the phone did in fact turn out to be very helpful. His inquiry was quickly answered with an affirmative,

James Whitmore had been dispatched to the county seat at about two forty five that morning to help troubleshoot a problem with the emergency response phone line. They also told him that as far as they knew, the problem hadn't been resolved until shortly after ten o'clock. James had called in to say that he wouldn't be leaving just yet because he had decided to have lunch in town before heading back.

Although it certainly sounded like a plausible alibi, he needed to be certain that James hadn't actually finished up hours ago and was simply lying to the dispatcher on the phone. He called the non-emergency number for the Emergency Management Office for the county and was routed to the dispatch supervisor. The supervisor confirmed that James had been there since very early that morning and had only left the facility in the last half hour.

Once again, he found himself right back at square one with no idea of who the villain was or what their motivation might be. Since James had a solid alibi but also knew Carla better than most people in town, he decided to try a different tactic. He called the phone company back and asked them to patch him through to James. When he got him on the phone, he immediately explained that Carla was missing and asked James if he had any idea who might want to harm her.

James was dumbfounded to think that anyone would want to hurt Carla, much less kidnap her; nor could he think of any possible motive. Wanting to do something to help with the investigation he promised Sam that he would head back immediately and said that it would probably take him about 45 minutes to get there. They agreed to meet at the police station as soon as James got back in town. In the meantime, Sam would call up the evidence technician to see if anything at all had turned up.

Sam's call to the technician provided some interesting details. It looked as though the dog had been killed before the struggle in the kitchen took place. The timeline was based on the fact that the dog's blood that had been tracked and smeared about by two people. At any rate, there were two different sets of footprints in one of the blood smears. The prints came from one person wearing shoes and a second who was barefoot. From the size of the barefoot print and a comparison with shoes in the bedroom closet, it was likely that they were made by Carla Barnes. That would mean that the footprint wearing the shoe came from whoever had taken Carla. It would also mean that it was very likely the dog had been killed to keep it quiet when the perpetrator entered the house. The print appeared to be from a woman's shoe, size eight.

That information sent Sam back over to talk to Suzanne. On his way out of his office, he grabbed the list of people who had been in the Barnes house that Carla had provided and that Suzanne had used for her previous background checks. She had lived in this town all of her life and knew most of the people in it far better than he did. When he walked over to her desk, she looked at him in surprise.

"Sam, I've only just gotten started and I haven't found anything relevant yet".

Sam's face was grim as he replied, "I didn't really expect that you had Suzanne. I need a different kind of information and I'm hoping you can help me out."

Suzanne was pleased that he would come to her for help and resolved to do whatever she could to help get rid of that grim expression.

"You know I'll do whatever I can to help you. What do you need?"

"I need you to take a look at this list again and highlight all of the women. Can you do that really quick while I wait? It's pretty urgent." She reached across the desk for the sheet of paper and scanned down it quickly while reaching for a red ink pen.

"Well this is easy; there are only nine women on the list. I've circled their names. Is that all you needed?"

"Just one more question and it's going to sound a little strange. Do you have any idea what size shoes any of them wear?" he handed the sheet back to her as a reference and looked at her hopefully.

Totally bemused by the question, Susanne took the sheet back from him and looked at it again.

"I can't say for sure what size most of them wear, but I can tell you that Harriet Cooper has really big feet and so does Jeannie Long. Moreover, I seem to recall that Susie Tooks has tiny feet. Does that help at all? Do you need me to try finding out what size feet they all have? I can give them all a call and ask, if that would help.

Sam nodded and gave her a wry smile. He thought for just a moment about how that conversation would go and it almost made him chuckle to imagine it,

"Hi Susie, it's Suzanne from the police station, would you mind telling me what size feet you have? Oh, no reason really, just trying to decide if you're a murderer or kidnapper. Thanks Susie goodbye."

Yeah, that was going to go over real well. Still, anything that might help eliminate a few names off the list would be really useful at this point.

"Sure Suzanne, but you have to promise to tell me later on how those phone calls went. I'll bet they're going to be interesting. Anyway, just so you know, I'm interested in anyone who wears a size eight. In the meantime, I'm expecting James Whitmore to show up here shortly. If you see him before I do would you send him my way?

She was already dialing the phone and gave him a slightly distracted nod as she picked up her pen to make notes on the list. Sam stopped by the break room and grabbed a cup of coffee in a Styrofoam cup and one of the leftover donuts somebody had brought in for breakfast that morning. It was apparent he wasn't going to get lunch anytime soon and he had a feeling that something was going to break on the case in fairly short order. Fortified with sugar and caffeine he headed back to his desk, meeting up with James just outside his office door.

THIRTEEN

My whole world had been rocked by the news from detective Gunne that somebody had apparently kidnapped Carla, not to mention the fact that they killed poor Flash in the process. Carla was a sweet lady and always willing to help out others, it just didn't make any sense at all to me that someone could mean her harm. I drove like a demon all the way back to Element, probably breaking at least a couple of dozen traffic laws along the way. To be perfectly honest I'm not sure I even remember most of the drive. I just kept trying to get my brain to understand what he had said. I had told him that it would take me about 45 minutes to get back but I made it in 30. I pulled up out front of the police station, slammed on the brakes, and jumped out of the car practically before it came to a stop. Once inside I ran into the detective just outside his office door. I remember noticing with some amazement that he was calm enough to be drinking coffee and munching doughnuts in the middle of a crisis.

I'm afraid I wasn't very polite to him and opened up the conversation with demands to know exactly what was going on; and what he accomplished so far; and what they had found so far and what they were doing to find Carla. In truth a lot of what I was asking, he couldn't tell me, or shouldn't have, since I wasn't a cop and it was an official investigation. It didn't stop me from asking and it didn't stop him from answering which was probably a good thing in the long run.

He explained to me what he knew so far.

Then he laid out the timeline of events as near as they had been able to establish it. I remember feeling a brief pang of sadness when he told me how Flash had died. He'd been a beautiful animal with a very loving disposition and with Gus gone; he had kept Carla from being all alone in the house. To think that someone had killed him just to keep him quiet was monstrous, but not quite as monstrous as what they might be doing or have done to Carla. I was really surprised when he said that it appeared to have been a woman. I honestly couldn't think of any woman that I knew who could cut a dog's throat in cold blood like that. Somehow, a size 8 shoe didn't seem like very much to go on. I don't know much about women's shoe sizes except that I remembered Sara complaining that stores were always running out of size 7 ½. If that was the most common size for women's shoe than a size 8 would be merely average as near as I could figure. I didn't think it would narrow the field very much.

He had just finished going over the details with me when Suzanne Mills showed up at his door.

"Oh I'm sorry, I don't mean to intrude. Detective Gunne, I have that information you asked for."

Sam let her know was okay to share the information with me as well, and so we learned that only two of the women on Carla's list at size 8 feet. Perhaps that clue was worth more than I was giving it credit for. On the other hand, it seems that both of the women that were size 8 shoes were over 70 years old. Not very good candidates for violent crimes and kidnapping to my mind.

We spent the next 20 minutes or so trying to figure out a reasonable way to expand the search without going around and checking every female foot in town in a perverse take off of Cinderella. We had pretty much run out of ideas, at least ideas that would work in the real world.

Sam and I spent a long time trying to figure things out and eventually had to concede that we just didn't have enough information to solve anything yet. There had to be some clue still at Carla's house that we hadn't gotten. I finally left the station at about two thirty and headed home to grab something to eat and clean up. After all, I had left the house before dawn and had been going flat out ever since.

I parked in front of the house and dragged myself inside, starting to feel the drain of too little sleep and too much stress. While my body was exhausted and wanted nothing more than to crash for about 3 days, my mind was in overdrive. I kept coming back to the fact that Carla was missing. At least she was ONLY missing and not dead. I had to tell myself that she wasn't dead. If she were dead, then why

take the body. There was no body found so that meant that she was still alive, right? It wouldn't make any sense for somebody to take her body and then leave the dog's body. At least not if they were trying to hide the crime.

Unfortunately, it also meant that we were probably running out of time. Whoever had taken her probably wouldn't keep her alive for too long. For one thing, keeping somebody prisoner and hiding it from the whole world for an extended period would be very difficult. The longer they kept her alive, the more chance that she would escape or that somebody would find her. Nor did I think it was realistic that she could possibly be held in town and kept secret. This meant that in order to keep her alive, either they had to stay wherever she was or keep returning on a regular basis to make sure she was still there, feed her (I hoped), etc. All of which came down to the fact that if she were still alive, it probably wouldn't be for more than a few hours or a day…two at most. Anything longer than that and the kidnapper's behavior would give them away.

Of course, that logic assumed that she had been taken by somebody in town. What if it was a stranger passing through town? Just somebody committing a random act? How could we ever find her then? The only hope we had was to believe that it was somebody local, somebody we knew. Problem was we had no idea who it was or why they had done it. It was probably the same person that had killed Gus, but that wasn't any help since half the town had been on the list of possible suspects. Carla's kidnapping had to be related but in what way? Was Gus killed to cause Carla pain or was Carla kidnapped because she had figured out who killed Gus and confronted them?

In a twisted way, it almost made sense to believe that Gus had been killed by somebody looking to make Carla suffer. When they decided that her pain wasn't great enough, they took her as well so that they could hurt her directly. How great would a person's hatred have to be for such actions and what could possibly trigger that much hate? Unfortunately, if the two incidents were linked, the only thing that it meant was that whoever had done it was quite willing to kill. Not a comforting thought at all.

I threw together a cold cut sandwich and poured a glass of iced tea. I really would rather have had a beer at that point but didn't want to do anything that might slow my reaction time if I needed to act fast. I took both upstairs and grabbed bites in between cleaning up and changing clothes. As I was pulling on a fresh tee shirt I looked out the window and saw Alex coming out of her house next door with a couple of large trash bags. The next day was trash pickup so it wasn't particularly surprising. She dumped the bags in the trash bin at the curb and headed back inside. I grabbed the empty glass and headed back downstairs. I dropped the glass in the sink on the way through the kitchen and headed out the side door towards Alex's house. I wanted to let her know what had happened and see if she had any ideas to add.

When she answered the door, she was dressed in skimpy grey shorts and a pink tank top tee shirt. For a moment she looked surprised to see me but one look at my face must have shown that something was wrong.

"James, I thought you were on a call. Come on inside." She turned and led the way towards the kitchen, looking back over her shoulder at me.

"I was just making some iced tea, would you like some?"

I followed her through the house unable to avoid noticing, even in the midst of all the stress and concern about Carla's kidnapping and figuring out who killed Gus, how well the meager outfit snuggled up to her generous curves. It really was a very impressive sight and certainly enough to distract me for the time it took to get from the front door to the kitchen. As I walked down the hallway, I remembered the night before. Strange to think it had been less than 24 hours. We had gotten back from dinner and retreated to the king size brass bed upstairs in my bedroom. The night had been intensely erotic and most definitely exhausting; another reason why I hadn't gotten any sleep the night before. My imagination created a vision of what was beneath her formfitting outfit this afternoon that certainly woke me back up.

A little bit disgusted with myself when I realized how easily distracted I was getting, I chalked it up to fatigue, and when she turned around at the counter, I explained my reason for stopping by. I don't think it was the one she was expecting after last night.

"Alex, I came over to tell you that Carla Barnes is missing. We think she might have been kidnapped by the same person that killed Gus. I just spent the last several hours with detective Gunne trying to figure out exactly what happened and where they might have taken Carla but we are at a dead-end."

Her reply was a bit irritated, "James, I thought we agreed that you wouldn't talk to the detective unless I was present. I cannot protect you from the consequences of anything you might say if I'm not there."

I spent the next couple of minutes explaining to her that I was absolutely not a suspect in Carla's disappearance; that even the detective had admitted there was no way I could have done it when I was physically in the presence of other people miles away at the time. My only involvement this time was as Carla's friend, someone who knew her well enough to perhaps fill-in a few gaps in Sam's knowledge which were caused simply by him being the new man in town. She accepted my answer but still seemed kind of annoyed with me so I decided to try a different tack.

"In addition to being worried about Carla, I'm also worried about you being here alone. Regardless of who did it and exactly what happened, the one thing we do know for sure is that there is someone on the loose who is willing to kill."

Making an instant decision even I was surprised by the next thing I said, had looking positively stunned.

Alex

"I think that maybe you should stay at my house. At least until we catch whoever it is that's doing these things. I would be a lot happier knowing I didn't have to worry about your safety."

Alex stood there, stared at me for a long moment, and then gave me a rather coy smile.

"Why James; that has got to be the nicest excuse for a proposition I've ever heard. It's certainly far more creative than the usual line and you tempt me to accept. Honestly though, I'm a big girl and I can take care of myself. You on the other hand look terrible; did you get any sleep at all after I left?"

"Alex I'm serious. There is a cold blooded killer loose in this town. We have no idea at all how he is picking his targets or what his motive might be. I've really don't like the idea of you being here all alone. If you won't stay at my place then get out of town for a few days until the police catch this guy."

She walked across the kitchen until we were toe to toe and then brought her hand up to gently touch my cheek.

"You're really serious aren't you? This isn't just an attempt to get me back into bed, is it?"

I reached up, put my hand over hers, and then brought her hand around so that I could plant a kiss on her knuckles. I looked down at her over our joined hands and brought the other hand around to rest at the small of her back.

"As delightful as the idea of going back to bed with you is, at the moment I really am serious. Stay with me, please?"

She leaned into me, responding to pressure of my hand against her back, and rested her head on my shoulder. We stayed like that for a long moment before she leaned back slightly so that she could look me in the eye.

"That has to be the most incredibly sweet offer I've ever had. I'm really, really tempted to take you up on it. Unfortunately, I have to head out to the county seat for a couple of days on business anyway. I had planned on leaving late this afternoon and staying up there overnight tonight so that I would be fresh first thing in the morning for a business meeting. So you see, you don't have to worry about me at all. I'll be safely tucked away from harm, far away from here until Wednesday. Besides, I'll bet you haven't slept at all since yesterday morning. The last thing you need is somebody else in your house keeping you awake. Will that satisfy your chivalrous instincts?"

"Actually, part of me is a bit disappointed; I think I was growing rather fond of the idea of being your knight in shining armor. Not to mention the potential fringe benefits of keeping you in my bed for your own protection." I chuckled, "but you're right. At the moment I'm so tired that I probably wouldn't be a very "entertaining" host. At least, not until I've gotten a few hours sleep."

She smiled and leaned in to give me a long lingering kiss that was almost enough to overcome my fatigue, before stepping away so that she was standing in front of me with her hands on her hips.

"Now that's settled, why don't you get some sleep? I have to finish assembling the stuff I need for my trip and then I'm out of here. I'm sure that if the detective needs your help in solving the case, he knows where to find you. You won't be any good to him or anyone else if you're dead on your feet. So...you rest, I'll lawyer, and I will see you in a couple of days. How does that sound?"

I had to admit that she made a lot of sense. I stepped forward and put an arm around her waist before turning towards the front of the house,

"Okay counselor, you win this round.

Rain check?"

Her answer was emphatic enough to make me regret going back to my own house but I knew she was right. I got back to my house and was shedding clothes on my way upstairs to bed. I don't even remember reaching the bedroom, but I woke up to the sound of the phone ringing.

FOURTEEN

After Whitmore left the station, Sam collected up all of their scribbled notes and walked over to see Suzanne. He was hoping she'd have a little time to sit down, look at things, and perhaps give him a fresh perspective. He had the feeling that he was missing something but he had looked at it all so many times that it was starting to get jumbled in his head and a fresh set of eyes might see things completely differently. It didn't hurt that it gave him an excuse to get to know Suzanne little better and spend some time with her. He hadn't really been interested in any woman since he had moved to this one horse town but he was beginning to think that he had been overlooking a gem just down the hall. It was certainly worth investigating when this was all over. The way she smiled at him when he walked into her office made him think that there might be hope after all.

Suzanne was pleased and flattered that the detective wanted her help on the case. He was so very different from anybody she had ever known before. Of course, she had spent all of her life here in Element, where the choices were somewhat limited. She had been really worried when he first joined the department; he was probably the worst burnout case that had ever passed through this town. Everyone had probably known why he moved here, the bad things that happened in big cities didn't happen in this town.

Now here he was, finally starting to act like he wanted to live again, and he had both a murder and a kidnapping to solve. She was a bit worried about the effect that it would have on him. Anything she could do to help him out was bound to be important, because the sooner this case was solved, the better off he would be in the long run.

He brought her up to speed on the disappearance of Carla Barnes. The two of them spent a couple of hours shoulder to shoulder at her desk as he walked her through everything that he knew about the kidnapping and all of the evidence, not that there was very much, that had been found so far. The idea being that she might be able to point out something he was missing or she might know something that he didn't about somebody here in town. It was a good idea; he hadn't lived here all that long and there was a lot of history that he just wasn't aware of. She had been able to fill in a few gaps in his knowledge about Gus Barnes and all the traveling he had done before he finally settled down to running the local hardware store. The whole town had known about James and Carla because there just really wasn't any way to keep a thing like that secret in a town where everybody was living in everyone else's hip pocket.

The affair hadn't lasted very long because it hadn't taken very long at all, before someone to let Gus know what was going on. As soon as that happened, he stopped traveling and stayed home. Of course, that is exactly what Carla had wanted all along anyway. James' reasons really would have not been much more complex as far as she knew; mostly he had just been reacting to sudden loneliness from the breakup of his marriage. As a result, the ending had apparently been polite and not particularly painful for either of them.

She had to admit that Sam seemed to have done an amazingly thorough job of analyzing the meager evidence as well as all of the potential motives. At least those that anyone knew about. The problem seemed to be that whatever the motivation was for killing Gus and kidnapping Carla (and her mind just kept insisting they had to be related) was either so far in the past that nobody but the killer remembered it anymore or it hadn't happened in Element at all. If it was simply so old that nobody remembered it, there was a chance that they could dig it up. On the other hand, if it had happened somewhere else, there was no way anybody in town could possibly help figure out what it was.

"Sam, the way I see it, if Carla is still alive, we have a limited amount of time to figure this out. That means we have to choose a direction to investigate. Either we spend the time digging deeper into the past of the people here in town, or we start looking outside for the motive. Unless we bring in outside help, I don't think we have time to do both quickly enough to save her. What do you think?"

Sam looked at her and raised his eyebrows in surprise, "What I think is that you have the makings of a good detective. I agree. Time is the key thing here and it's something we don't have a lot of. I'm impressed. So tell me, which way do you think I should go? You know the people in this town a lot better than I do, if you had to choose what would you do?"

She tilted her head and looked up at him, noticing for the first time the slightly spicy cologne that he was wearing. It was a pleasant sensation to have someone as knowledgeable and experienced as him ask her for advice. She thought carefully before she spoke, determined not to let him down.

"Most of the people in town have lived here all their lives, not very many new folks move into this town. That means that there are fewer outsiders to investigate than long-term residents. That could be an advantage. On the other hand, it also means needing information from other places that might not be available so easily. Internet searches are handy but they certainly won't tell you everything. You have to understand that I'm just kind of thinking out loud right now. If we are looking for a woman with size 8 feet, and we're trying to decide if it's a woman who has lived here a long time or someone with relatively new to the area, I would start with the women who haven't lived here very long. At least it's a place to start while we wait to see if the evidence technician turns up anything new. I also think we better pray that they do, because without more evidence I'm not sure we can solve it soon enough to do Carla Barnes any good."

It was as good a plan as any other and beat the hell out of just flipping a coin. When she offered to compile a list of women that had moved here from other places and reference it with Carla's list of visitors, she asked how far back to go. After a bit of discussion, it was decided to go back until Gus Barnes High School years. Twenty five years, give or take a couple should be far enough; at least they hoped it would. He left her to work on the list while he checked with the evidence technician to see if anything new had been gleaned from the crime scene. As he left her office, he stopped in the doorway and turned around,

"Suzanne, I really appreciate your help. You've been great."

His words elicited a blinding smile that nearly took his breath away and for a moment, he had trouble remembering where he had been headed.

"Flatterer, Go check with the technician, I should be done by the time you get back."

Sam sat at his desk for a couple of minutes reflecting on the chance encounter that had brought him to Element and introduced him to such an interesting woman. Finally giving himself a mental shake, he called the evidence technician's cell phone. His request for an update was met with enthusiasm.

"Detective, I was almost ready to call you. I found a couple of things that might interest you. First of all, from the drying pattern of the blood and the path of the footprints, I would say that the dog was killed within minutes before the footprints were made. It doesn't' look like the blood had time to start drying and in fact may still have been spreading when it was walked through. Since the bloody footprints lead across the room to where the table and chairs were pushed around and overturned, it looks like the struggle took place after the dog was killed. Secondly, the door either wasn't locked or the intruder had a key. There was no damage to the lock itself and no scratch marks around the keyhole. There is no way to be sure if it the back door was locked but the front door was; doesn't really make much sense to lock the front door but not the back door, does it."

"Wait, wait just a minute. Are you telling me that whoever took Carla Barnes might have had a key to the house? That has to be a pretty short list of people, I would think. I'm not sure how to use it since we don't know who in town may have been given a key, but it's something to go on. Anything else?"

FIFTEEN

Carla woke up and found herself in the dark. Her hands and feet had been bound together and there was something that felt like tape covering her mouth. She could feel the rough texture of soil against the skin of her cheek, what were probably small pebbles, and chunks of earth pressing into her skin everywhere it touched the ground. In those first moments, as she regained consciousness, she was terrified by a certainty that she had been buried alive. She struggled furiously against the ties that held her but wasn't able to break free. Finally, exhausted, even more battered by having practically beaten herself senseless against the cold hard dirt, she lay still, breathing as best she could through her nose. As the initial panic gave way to exhausted defeat, she tried to remember what had happened and how she had ended up in this situation.

She had been sound asleep when a noise downstairs woke her up. It was gone almost as quickly as it had come and in the groggy moments as she was waking up, she began to doubt that she had actually heard anything. She lay there for a couple of minutes, listening hard for any additional noise and eventually thought she heard a thump from someplace near the kitchen. She looked over at the clock on the bedside table and groaned. It was only three fifteen in the morning.

Deciding that what she had heard was probably Flash getting into the kitchen trash again she got out of bed muttering about animals that had no consideration for people who wanted to sleep. She really hadn't been sleeping all that well since Gus died. She had never been able to sleep properly when he wasn't beside her.

It was no different these days, although she assumed that she would eventually get past the feeling that he might be home soon. In the meantime, she savored any chance to get some rest. Being woken up in the middle of the night by the darn dog was just seriously irritating. It didn't help that she had been well aware that the trash should go out before she went to bed. Gus had taken care of that little chore religiously for her, knowing Flash's tendency to go trashcan diving at night. She really should have done it last night but she kept forgetting that she had to do it herself from now on.

She rolled out of bed and got dressed in sweatpants and a sweatshirt. Sleep was gone now; she might just as well get up. By the time she got downstairs and cleaned up the trash, she would be wide awake and thoroughly annoyed at the dog. There was no way she would be able to get back to sleep anytime soon.

Tramping down the stairs, she called out to Flash, making dire promises about getting a doghouse and parking it in the backyard for him. She recalled thinking that it was a bit unusual for him not to come running when she called his name but decided that he probably knew he was in trouble and was looking for a small, dark corner to hide in. Of course, being a fair sized dog, there weren't many reasonable hiding places in the house for him. She continued to call for him as she made her way down the hall towards the back of the house where the kitchen was located.

Still no sign of Flash and it was beginning to make that little voice in the back of her mind whisper in concern. As she neared the kitchen door, she saw a shiny dark stain on the floor in the moonlight that streamed through the window. A couple of more steps brought Flash into view. He was lying on the floor. In the dim light she could see a pool of black oozing out from underneath him and spreading out across the cream colored tiles like a tide of death.

She cried out his name and ran towards him hoping that there was something she could do to save him. Even as she ran, she knew from the amount of blood on the floor that it was too late. Just a couple of steps from the body of her poor dog, something had hit her in the back. It propelled her forward into the side of the kitchen table, knocking over a chair and sending her staggering though the pool of blood, her bare feet slipping in the warm ooze.

The next thing she had known, she was waking up, her hands bound and tape over her mouth to prevent her from screaming, by somebody behind her who was trying to pull her upright. An attempt to struggle away from the grasping hands had brought a quick motion from behind and the feel of a sharp metal edge against her throat. She instantly went still allowing herself to be pulled up to her feet by the unseen hands. She glanced once to the side and in the silver moonlight, she could see the gaping wound on Flash's neck, it was obviously fatal and told her that her unseen assailant wasn't at all hesitant to kill if they wanted to. Her only hope of survival would come from cooperating as long as possible in hopes of rescue. When the hands shoved her towards the back door, she stumbled forward, trying not to fall over again.

They had gone out the back door and around the side of the house where she saw the open trunk of a dark sedan. In the available light, she thought it might be dark blue or black. She thought to look at the license plate in an attempt to memorize it but only caught the first three letters. It seemed familiar but she couldn't be sure. Then the hands pushed her into the trunk and shoved her head down against the floor before slamming it closed.

The car drove for what seemed like hours but probably wasn't. There was no way to know how long she had been in the trunk, being bounced around as the car navigated the rough roads, hitting potholes and such at what seemed to be a pretty fast speed. Eventually the sound of the tires on the road changed and the ride became rougher and she decided that they had left the paved surface and turned onto a dirt road. The car bounced along for a while, the road seeming to twist and turn, leaving her bruised and battered from being tossed around.

The whole time the car was traveling, she was trying to figure out what to do, how to save herself from whatever the person who had kidnapped her might have planned. She thought of turning over so that she could see their face when they opened the trunk, but then she thought that perhaps seeing their face would mean that they would kill her for sure, simply because she could identify who they were. On the other hand, she was very afraid that whoever it was planned to kill her anyway, or why else would they be taking her so far out off the beaten path to whatever isolated place they were headed.

A truly horrible thought came to her…what if they didn't open the trunk. What if they planned to push the car into a river with her inside? They didn't even have to do that; they might drive the car out into the woods and set it on fire to destroy the evidence. She was so afraid at that point that she couldn't think straight anymore. The idea of drowning or being set on fire horrified her. She writhed in terror, trying desperately to escape.

Eventually, logic reasserted itself and she decided that as long as she was alive, there was a chance. She just had to start thinking straight and try to save herself if she could.

She tried to find some rough edge inside the trunk that she might be able to use to cut the tape around her wrists. Perhaps, if she could get loose, she could surprise them when they opened the trunk lid and get away. After a long time squirming around, trying to feel the inside of the trunk with her hands bound behind her, she did find a bit of rough metal and began to try to slash through the several layers of tough tape. Unfortunately, before she could finish the car skidded to a stop and footsteps came around the back. She heard the sound of a key, scraping in the lock and then the trunk popped open.

After being in the dark for so long, her eyes took a moment to adjust and before she could get a clear look at her assailant, they drew something dark and baglike over her head, effectively blindfolding her. Hands grabbed her upper arms and pulled her into a sitting position, draping her legs over the edge of the trunk opening and pulling her to her feet. She swayed for a moment, dizzy from the sudden change in position and disorientation of the blindfold, then was guided away from the car.

She staggered along for what seemed like forever, stumbling over rough ground and tripping over what may have been tree roots, all the while aware of the occasional touch of the knife blade that was used to let her know that she was in serious trouble. Twice she fell and was hauled back to her feet before being forced to continue. The rocks and roots tore at her bare feet and it hadn't taken very long before she was limping, badly. Before the journey ended she had been whimpering with pain at every step.

She had eventually been guided up three steps and across a wooden floor. The relative smoothness of the wood under her feet was sweet relief after the nightmare trek through the woods. The hands had let go for a brief moment, during which she heard the sound of furniture moving and rusty hinges creaking, then they had returned. The bag was ripped off and she was suddenly blinded by the light.

She was standing in the middle of a rustic looking wooden building. In front of her was a large opening in the floor, created by the trap door that had been propped open. The thought ran through her mind that the trapdoor opening had probably been the source of the noisy hinges. She was turned around roughly and finally saw the face of her tormentor; just before she was pushed backwards into the gaping hole in the floor. Her initial shocked amazement was obliterated by the sensation of falling and then consciousness vanished as her head hit the floor of the chamber below.

SIXTEEN

In the end, I only slept for a couple of hours before I woke up dreaming about finding Carla just in time to have her die in my arms. It didn't take a psychiatrist to tell me that the dream was an echo of Sara's death and that I was afraid of losing somebody close again. Even Freud would have found my analysis reasonable. Wide awake, I gave up and got dressed then headed back down to the police station. When I arrived, Sam was on the phone with the evidence technician getting an update. He saw me coming towards him and punched the speaker button on the phone.

"I found a couple of long blond hairs caught in the latch on the side gate. I'll have to get them back to the lab for further testing, but I can tell you that they are about 18 inches long and appear to have root tags. With luck, a DNA lab may be able to match them, if you can get a reference sample from a suspect."

Sam almost came up out of his chair at the news. At last, another solid piece of evidence to work from! Something that might lead them directly to the perpetrator. He thanked the technician and hung up, sprinting down the hallway to Suzanne's office. He came skidding to a halt just in time to avoid running straight into her as she came through the doorway, a piece of paper in her hand. They ended up practically nose-to nose, both of them a bit breathless. She spoke first,

"I have the list of names for you. There are only a couple of dozen women that moved into town in the past twenty-five years and not all of them are still here."

"Terrific! Can you tell me if any of them are blonds?

When he had asked her if she could think of any women that lived in or near town and had long blonde hair, well past shoulder length, she looked bemused. She sat there and thought about it for a few moments, then got up and left the room saying she'd be right back. When she returned several minutes later, she had with her the only hairdresser in town. Her shop was just two doors up the block from the station. If anybody in town knew who had long blonde hair, it would be her.

Sam seemed impressed by her ingenuity and I was impressed by just how attentive Sam was to Suzanne. It seemed to me like there was a potential for something more to develop. The two women put their heads together and in fairly short order had produced a list of perhaps 15 or so names of women with the right hairstyle. It was then a process of elimination to tentatively cross off the list those who were too young, too old, or otherwise physically unlikely to have committed the crime. That cut the list down by about half. Crosschecking those remaining with the list Carla had provided dropped the number to four.

For a moment we were back to going around measuring women's feet. Sam and I were about ready to break out our handsome prince suits and go searching for our evil Cinderella when one of the names on the list jumped out at me. It was Alexandra Kincaid.

No, that just wasn't possible. What possible motive could Alex have to hurt Carla?

There had to be another explanation, a reason for those hairs caught on the gate. Maybe they had been there for a while...maybe they had gotten caught there while she was taking care of Flash back at the beginning of the summer. On the other hand, perhaps she had been there some other time since then. A couple of stray hairs didn't have to mean anything. We didn't even know for sure that the kidnapper was on Suzanne's list, it could have been somebody that had lived in town forever. There was no way I was going to believe that Alex could have done this, it just didn't make any sense at all.

I looked over at Sam and Suzanne and felt a cold knot of fear growing in my stomach. I looked back at the list and knew that Alex made as much sense as any other name written on that stupid sheet of paper. I guess that Sam must have seen the look on my face because he took the list from my limp hand and scanned it and then he looked up at me and said exactly what I had been dreading.

"Alex Kincaid."

I shook my head at him, mutely trying to deny what my gut was already starting to believe.

"But WHY? What possible reason could she have for killing Gus OR taking Carla? It doesn't make any sense."

Sam looked hard at me and shrugged, "Maybe it's her, but we only have four names on this list to check out and none of them have any motive that I know of. We have to start someplace and she is just as good as any other name here. Maybe what happened to Gus and what happened to Carla aren't related. Maybe the motives are completely different."

He turned to look at Suzanne, "I'm going to need another background check, and Alex is one name that we never seriously considered before. Can you check her out? Can you do it right now, starting with Alexandra Kincaid? In the meantime, I think James and I need to have a little chat."

Suzanne quickly agreed and then shooed us out of her office so that she could get to work. Sam and I went back to his office and sat down.

"James, what do you know about Alexandra Kincaid? You probably know her about as well as anybody since you live right next door to her. What do you know about her background?"

I filled him in on what I knew; that she had grown up in Kansas City, mostly in foster care, that her mother had been an alcoholic and a crack addict. That she had never known her father. I told him about how she had put herself through school and had moved here to get away from all the violence and the bad memories of where she had grown up. He stopped me for a moment to call Suzanne on the internal phone line,

"For Alex Kincaid, focus your search on Kansas City and include her mother if you can, OK?"

After getting an affirmative answer from the other end of the line, he hung up the phone and gestured for me to continue.

I wrapped up my narrative amidst internal prayers that it was somebody...anybody...but Alex. She had been good to me but even more importantly, she had been good FOR me. I had been pretty withdrawn since Sara's death and Alex had begun to draw me out again. The last couple of days had been pretty good ones for me and I was looking forward to that continuing. When I wound down, Sam asked when I had last seen Alex and I realized that this was the piece of information I was looking for to justify my faith in her. She had been home today. If she had kidnapped Carla early in the morning, wouldn't she have been away from the house? She had certainly been acting as if nothing was out of the ordinary. I couldn't imagine a kidnapper calmly inviting me in and trying to seduce me at the same time they were in the middle of the kidnapping. It just wasn't possible.

It was about then that Suzanne buzzed Sam's intercom and said that she had something to show him. I tagged along behind him as he walked over to see her and so I was there then she told him that she had been unable to find anything on Alexandra Kincaid. Not even a birth record. It was as if she had never existed before the day she moved to Element.

Sam and I were stunned but he recovered first.

"Are you saying that she isn't who she claims to be?"

Suzanne nodded at him, looking a bit embarrassed at having dropped such momentous news on him.

"That's exactly what I'm saying. The Division of Motor Vehicles doesn't have a record of a driver's license under that name, or a car registration for that fact. The phone company records show that there is no phone in that house, the phone number you gave for her is one of those pay as you go cell phones. It has her name on it but companies don't do any kind of check on your identity when you buy one of those. You can even buy them at convenience stores."

It made no sense. There had to be some record of her, she drove a car, she had to have a driver's license. Didn't she? The car had to be registered to somebody, didn't it? My mind went into overdrive at that point, thinking of all the different things that a name had to be used for, that you have to provide to prove your identity on a daily basis. You can't open a bank account without proof of identity; have electricity, gas, telephone service. For that fact, she owned the house she was living in, didn't she? Maybe not, maybe it was a rental. Either way, you have to prove who you are to sign the paperwork. Hell, you can't even use a credit card to buy groceries without proof of identity.

"Suzanne, is there any record of who owns the house she is living in? I mean, somebody has to own that place, if it isn't her, maybe it's somebody that can lead us to her."

Sam looked at me and seemed impressed. "That's a good question. Suzanne, can you check the ownership of that property?"

"Sure thing Sam, give me just a minute. I can check the county tax site to see who is listed as the owner of record on the tax bill."

We hovered over her shoulder for the five or six minutes it took her to log into the county government web site and check the tax records, neither of us willing to say anything. For me, the main thought that kept repeating over and over inside my mind was; who the hell had I slept with the night before? I really didn't get much beyond that question when Suzanne came up from behind her computer monitor.

"Well, this just gets odder and odder. That house is listed as being owned by Gus Barnes."

Both of us goggled at her in amazement. If this case could

have gotten any more twisted, her words were just about the only way it could have happened. Why would she have been living in a house owned by Gus Barnes? How come nobody seemed to know that Gus owned it? I started to get a nasty idea of just how warped she really was and decided to go with it.

"Can you tell us how long the house has belonged to Gus? I know that before Alex moved in it belonged to old Mrs. Foster. It wasn't long after she died that Alex moved in so I always assumed that she bought it from Mrs. Foster's estate. I know the old lady didn't have any family so the house logically would have gone on the market."

Suzanne disappeared behind the monitor again and Sam looked at me, "What's on your mind James? You look like you've had a revelation."

"I think that she was out for Gus long before she moved to town. For whatever reason, I think she moved here because of him in the first place. She is a lawyer after all and one of her specialties is real estate. How hard would it have been for her to fix it so that the property showed up in the records in his name? I have no idea why she would do that, but I think that is exactly what she did."

Suzanne popped back into view, "You're right James. The tax record shows that property tax changing directly from Mrs. Foster to Gus Barnes."

Sam's expression was incredulous. "So, either Gus bought the property and allowed her to live there, which would imply some kind of relationship between them, or she fixed the sale to put the house in his name without his knowledge. I'm not sure which one strikes me as stranger. Either way, I think I better call Judge Wells and get a couple of warrants, one to search her house and another for her arrest."

"You might want to add a third one if you can convince him of it. Alex told me that she owns a cabin up by Miller's Creek. I've got a nasty feeling in my gut. I think that's where she took Carla. I have no idea where it is, but if she told the truth, you probably need to check that out as well."

Sam decided not to wait for the warrant before heading over to Alex's house. He asked Suzanne to arrange for somebody to pick up the warrants from Judge Wells as soon as they were ready, then he called the Judge. He was on his cell phone to that worthy gentleman as he left the building and got into his car.

Sam drove his car and I drove mine so that I could drop it back by my house. There is probably some police rule that says he shouldn't have allowed me to come along on his investigation, but I lived right next door so there was no way that he could stop me from driving to my own home. I pulled up in the driveway and saw that Alex's car wasn't there. She had said that she was going up to the county seat for a couple of days but I figured that was just one more lie. I parked the car and walked over to her front porch. Sam tried to tell me that we had to wait for the warrant, but I pointed out to him that I was a private citizen and didn't need a warrant to pay a call on a neighbor, especially one that I had been sleeping with. I walked up the front steps and rang the doorbell while he waited on the front sidewalk, shaking his head in annoyance at my highhanded meddling in his investigation. There was no answer, which didn't surprise me since I knew she was out of town, so I decided to try the door anyway. It wasn't locked. I thought that was pretty strange considering the lecture she had given me on always locking the house before I left.

Before Sam could stop me, I opened the door and went on in the house calling for Alex. I was met by silence. Unlike Carla's house, there was no sign that there was anything wrong other than the unlocked door. Everything seemed to be neat and tidy, just as it had been when I was there early that afternoon. Everything seemed unremarkable on the first floor so I went upstairs to check the bedrooms.

I had never been upstairs in Alex's house before and I

felt a little bit uncomfortable wandering around the bedrooms until I opened the door to one of the spare bedrooms and stuck my head inside looking to see if she was there. I couldn't believe my eyes. I didn't think the detective was going to believe it either. Careful not to touch anything, I backed out of the room. I was headed for the front door when I met Sam on his way in. He had the warrant in his hand but stopped in his tracks when he saw my face. I was shaking hard by that time. "Sam, you better get up there. I think you just got the break you've been looking for on this case."

"Why? What did you find?"

I just shook my head and motioned for him to head up the stairs. "Second door on the right Sam. I think that Alex is seriously living out there in some other dimension. You're going to have to see it for yourself because you won't believe it if I just tell you."

He stepped past me and I turned to follow him back up the stairs, both mind and heart numb at the realization that Alex was apparently a complete sociopath, capable of doing pretty much anything while smiling at you the whole time.

The spare bedroom looked like something out of some Hollywood horror movie about an obsessed serial killer. In this case, the obsession was Gus Barnes. There were pictures of him everywhere, not only here in town but some of them were old enough to have been taken years ago when he was still doing a lot of traveling for his job. There were newspaper clippings of every article in the local paper that had ever mentioned his name; there were pictures of him walking with Flash and other pictures of him with Carla. There were also pictures of the inside of their house. Every room had been photographed from every angle. It was obvious that they had been taken by somebody who had a lot of time in the house. Time when nobody else was around.

"Sam…"

He looked over at me and raised a brow, "Looking at

these pictures of the inside of their house just reminded me. Alex was dog sitting for Gus and Carla back in May for over a week. She had all the time in the world to poke through every corner of their house and make her plans. She also had a key so she could take care of Flash. I'll bet she made a copy of that key before she gave it back. She could have been in and out of the house any time she wanted since then."

He looked as stunned as I felt.

"As meticulous as she is, she probably did look in every drawer and cabinet, including the refrigerator in the garage. She knew where he kept his insulin and could have tampered with it any time she wanted. She probably waited a while to be sure that nobody would connect her with it. After all, she had apparently been waiting for years; why not wait a few more weeks to be sure that everything went according to plan."

We went back to looking over the pictures and notes that papered the walls and desktop. I kept my hands in my pockets to help resist the temptation to pick things up to see what was underneath.

Without touching anything, I couldn't tell if there might be something that explained why Alex had been obsessed with Gus. However, obsession was the only word for what we were seeing. And while there didn't seem to be anything, at least on the surface, that would explain his murder, it did seem obvious that Alex had been stalking him for a very long time and probably was the one who had killed him.

Other than some pictures of Carla and Gus together, there didn't seem to be anything that pointed to why she would have killed Flash and taken Carla.

SEVENTEEN

Sam decided to head up towards Miller's Creek while Suzanne tried to identify from property records, the exact location of Alex's cabin. All I knew was that she had said it was about a mile off of Miller's Creek. Unfortunately, the creek wandered on a drunken path for miles through mountainous terrain. Most of the area wasn't accessible by car, so people generally either hiked or rode horses. A few intrepid souls rode ATVs but we were afraid that using them would make too much noise and alert her to our approach. The same thing could be said for landing a helicopter anywhere in the area. Just about the only thing we had going for us was the element of surprise and we couldn't afford to give up that advantage.

We were hoping that Suzanne could give us good directions once we got up to the area. She still had to figure out where it was, not an easy thing to do when Alex wasn't her real name and we already knew that she had put her own house in Gus' name to confuse the records. At the moment, we had no idea whose name to look for in the property records. Suzanne was resorting to searches of any property that had changed hands in the last 5 years on an assumption that Alex had pre- planned everything.

Alex already had about three hours head start and we had no idea what she might be doing to Carla while we were trying to figure out which way to look. I was scared silly that we would get there too late. The more I thought about everything, the angrier I got. I could only believe that she had seduced me to provide herself with an alibi. That's not very flattering when you stop to think about it.

Sam was driving and so I didn't have anything to do but sit there and think about all that had happened in the past few days. We still had no idea why Alex was obsessed with Gus Barnes or what had motivated her to abduct Carla, we only knew that there was a pretty high probability that she had. The incredible scene we had found in her house, with the hundreds of photos of Gus, the fact that she had apparently been stalking him at least since she moved to Element three years ago, if not a whole lot longer, all pointed to her as the most likely suspect for everything.

For me, the trip was a nightmare. I spent a lot of it wondering what clue I had missed that might have prevented Carla's kidnapping. It didn't help that Sam had the opinion that the kidnapping was more of a crime of opportunity than part of her obsession with Gus. I kept coming back to the fact that she must have been planning it while she was in bed with me. That the whole time we were together, that incredibly erotic night I spent with her, as well as the time we had spent together that afternoon. All the time she had been cold-bloodedly either planning the kidnapping or concealing it. I can tell you, it didn't do much for my ego. What had been probably the most passionate encounter I had ever experienced had crumbled to ashes for me.

I kept thinking that there must have been some sign, some clue to what was going on and that I had just missed it. If Carla died, it would be the second time in a year that a woman I cared about died because of me. I wasn't sure that I would ever be able to recover if that happened.

When we first got on the road, Sam tried to talk to me, telling me that he wanted me to stay out of the way and well back from the scene until he called for me. He had this theory that my relationship with Alex might allow me to talk to her if things got too tense. He wanted me to stall her until reinforcements arrived. I just wanted to be where I might be able to help Carla if I could. Staying at home waiting for news would have driven me mad under the circumstances. I owed it to everyone to do something to intervene because I should have known that Alex was psychotic.

Exactly how I was supposed to know was irrelevant, I should be able to tell if I'm in bed with a sociopath, shouldn't I? Unless...perhaps she had a split personality? Perhaps there was one personality which was a normal person (the one that seduced me) and one that was a cold-blooded killer. Great, I thought glumly. Add that to the ever growing list of possibilities, with no way to know if any of them were right or not.

We had made it all the way to Route Eight and were fast approaching the point where we were going to have to choose which direction to go at the fork before Sam's cell phone rang. We pulled over to the shoulder, the little caravan of police vehicles with backup officers pulled over behind us to wait for instructions from Sam. He spoke to her for a couple of minutes, occasionally saying things like, "that's OK Suzanne," and "every bit of information helps". He grabbed a note pad and pen out of his shirt pocket and started scribbling notes. Eventually he thanked her and told her to let him know if she found out anything new then hung up.

He nodded for me to get out of the car and we walked back to the other two vehicles, squinting against the brilliance of their headlights, to confer with the rest of the officers that were providing backup. Sam leaned against the first cruiser and crossed his arms as he spoke.

"Okay guys, here's the deal. Suzanne wasn't able to identify exactly which property Alex might be at. There are three places up there that changed hands in the last several years. We are going to assume that she is probably at one of them and split to check them all. All radios on ear buds and cell phones on vibrate; we don't want to let her know we are coming if we can help it. If you see her or think you might have the right cabin, don't intervene unless you believe that there is an imminent threat to Carla Barnes. Otherwise, call me and let me know your location. We don't want to do anything what will spook this woman into taking out the hostage. Remember that, this is a rescue operation, not just an arrest. This woman has a relationship with James here, so he is our best chance of talking her into releasing her victim. I would prefer a hostage negotiator, but we don't have one, so he is our next best tool in this situation. When we find the right location, I don't want any action taken until he is

131

handy to help us talk to her."

He turned to look at me, "I don't want you taking any chances either James. If we find them, you talk to her. Just talk, don't try to do something heroic, you understand me? Stay behind a tree if you can, because we don't know if she has a gun or not and I don't want her shooting you."

I smiled grimly at him and nodded, but deep inside I thought I might prefer for her to put me out of my misery if Carla was already dead. I wasn't about to tell him that, he would probably dump me on the side of the road right here and make me walk back to town if he thought I might do something stupid.

Sam laid a map of the general area out on the hood of the car and turned his flashlight on it. He drew three circles on the map to show the three target cabins. It turned out that there was a fair amount of distance between the three locations. After a couple of more minutes of discussion, Sam and I took the middle one. At least that way, we hoped to cut down our response time if it turned out to be one of the other two sites. We piled back into the vehicles and turned north on route 8. A couple miles up the road, we reached the gravel parking area at the end of the pavement. Alex's dark blue Camaro was parked in the darkest corner, under some trees. At least now we knew that she had lied about the business trip and that we were headed in the right direction.

After checking phones, flashlights, weapons (in the case of everybody else but me) we split into three teams and headed off on the trails back into the woods. I leaned nearer to Sam and whispered a question about how far in the cabin was. He looked at me and smiled in the moonlight.

"You don't have to whisper just yet James.

It's a couple of miles up this trail to the area of the cabin. When we get closer we will have to try to be as quiet as possible, but right now, I doubt her hearing is quite that good."

I continued to whisper, "I think you might be making a bad assumption Sam. We already know that she is tremendously organized and has resources we didn't know about. What's to say that she doesn't have some kind of security system surrounding the property?"

He stopped and turned to look me in the eye.

"James, I'm really sorry about Alex. I know that you were starting to get close to her. I don't think I've ever worked on a case before where the primary suspect's lawyer turned out to be the perp. That has to be a first of some kind. But hey, look on the bright side."

I remember thinking with a sense of wonder, „there's a bright side to all this?'

He grinned at me, "Just think of what could have happened if she hadn't decided that she liked you. She could have seriously trashed any chance for your defense…"

Not quite sure if I felt any better at that thought, I just turned and headed on up the trail. I kept thinking that there was something wrong, something that was hovering just beyond conscious thought that was important, but it kept slipping away. We trudged through the forest in silence for a long time before I realized what was bugging me. Why weren't we using dogs to track Alex's scent? This is hunting country and half the people in the county owned hunting dogs. At the very least, they would have told us which of the three locations our target was. I couldn't believe that we had missed such a simple solution to finding them. A seasoned veteran like Sam should have thought of that, or else one of the locally grown officers should have. For that matter, I should have thought of it a lot earlier than this. I really shouldn't be second guessing professionals this way, maybe they had thought of using dogs but had decided that they were too likely to have made noise and given us away. Maybe they had just been caught up in things the same way that I had been. Either way, I had to trust that they knew what they were doing.

After about a mile and a half I began to notice some dark spots in the rather sandy soil of the trail. They looked black and gleamed wetly in the moonlight. I stooped down and touched one of them only to have my finger come away with a spot of darkness. Sam crouched down next to me and turned the beam of his flashlight on my fingertip and then on the ground between us.

There was a dark red, almost black substance in the dirt, possibly dried blood. We looked at each other and then looked closer at the ground where the drop had been.

"It looks like a footprint from a bare foot. We know that Carla was barefoot when she left the house. I think we are on the right trail now.

"It looks like maybe she cut her foot on the way through the woods. The good news is; that means she was alive and walking on her own when they came through here."

"Are you going to call the other men and tell them to move this way?"

"No, just in case this came from a hiker who cut their hand or something, I think we better let them continue until somebody actually finds something more definitive. This looks promising but there is always a chance that this is unrelated. I prefer to hedge my bets as much as possible."

I agreed with him and we headed further down the trail, keeping our eyes open for any additional clues. Blood drops continued to appear in the dirt every few steps, reassuring me that we were headed in the right direction, even if the Detective didn't want to make any assumptions. All of a sudden, we came around a bend in the trail and saw the first signs of a building, a light gleaming from inside a small log cabin among the trees. It was set back from the trail by a couple of hundred yards. If it had been daytime, we might have missed it altogether, but in the dark, the light came peeking through between the trees like the beacon from a lighthouse guiding ships into port.

Deciding it was now time to be a lot more cautious, we toggled off our flashlights and stepped off the path into the trees. There we paused for a long time straining to see any hint of movement in the vicinity but there was none. We still weren't sure if it was even the right cabin since we hadn't actually seen either woman anywhere around. It looked like we were going to have to sneak up to the house and try to see inside in order to be sure.

We spent the next several minutes skulking carefully along through the undergrowth, trying not to step on any dry twigs, a skill apparently neither of us had ever mastered. We did our best and hopefully managed not to sound too much like a pair of bears thrashing through the woods in search of picnic baskets. We eventually worked our way up to the side of the house where we could stand in the shadows and peak in a window. What we saw was an unoccupied living room. The scene wasn't very helpful until I noticed a couple of bloody footprints in the doorway coming in from the porch and a windbreaker thrown over the back of a chair that looked an awful lot like one I had seen Alex wearing in the past.

It was enough to convince Sam that we probably had found the right location so he headed back down the trail a little ways to call the other two teams for backup. I continued to look around hoping to find some clue about where Carla was. After a few minutes, my curiosity got the better of me and I went around to the front of the house, across the front porch, and walked into the living space. Being careful to walk as quietly as possible, I wandered through the cabin. Of course being an amateur I'm not sure would've recognized a clue unless it jumped out and bit me. I eventually ended up back in the middle of the living room, at a complete loss for what to do next. That's when I heard a muffled noise coming from somewhere in or near the house.

It almost sounded like it was coming from underneath

the house but that didn't make much sense. I hadn't seen any sign that there might be a basement or even a crawl space. I went back outside and walked completely around the structure but it appeared to be built flat on the ground and there was certainly no exterior entrance that seemed to lead underneath it. It had been quite a bit since Sam had left to call in the reserves and I was beginning to wonder what had happened to him. I didn't go looking for him though because I was far more concerned with trying to find Carla. I went back inside the cabin and stood in the middle of the living room trying to hear the noise again.

There it was again, a barely audible noise that seemed to becoming from somewhere over on my right. I walked over to that side of the room and noticed, as I walked across a woven area rug, that the floor seemed to have a little bit of a bounce to it in the middle of the rug. I stamped by foot firmly and heard a little hollow sound. I knelt down and pulled back the rug. There was a trap door underneath the rug with a small notched area that provided a way to grip the door in order to lift it.

When I lifted the trap door up there was a short set of wooden stairs going down into what was apparently a root cellar. I flicked on my flashlight and aimed the beam down into the pitch black of the hole. To my horror, the beam illuminated what appeared to be the body of Carla Barnes lying tied up on the dirt floor. I went a little weak at the knees and cried out her name. She opened her eyes, blinking in the sudden light.

Something hit me hard right between the shoulder blades and I pitched forward into the root cellar striking my head on the dirt floor as the trap door slammed shut overhead. I must've passed out for a few minutes because when I came to Carla had managed to squirm around until her head was next to mine. Not that she could have done much to help me with both hands and feet bound by duct tape and another piece over her mouth. I had seen that much before being pushed into this pit and now I knew that her face was near mine because I could feel her breath and hear her muffled sobs through the tape, even though I couldn't see her in the utter darkness of the cellar.

I waited for the dizziness caused by hitting my head and waking up in darkness to settle down a bit. Once it had, I reached up and started trying to work loose the tape that was covering Carla's mouth, wincing at the pain I knew I had to be causing as I worked to pull the duct tape loose. As I worked on it, I kept telling her not to worry, that it was almost over, that detective Gunne knew we were here and that he had backup on the way, we would be free any minute now. I don't even remember everything I said, mostly I was just talking because I wanted to reassure her and also because the sound of my voice provided some kind of a reference point in the darkness. The more I talked, the more agitated she seemed to become. She was crying; her whole body wracked with shudders in what I assumed to be relief at knowing rescue was on the way. It was an assumption that she shattered when I finally worked free the last bit of tape from her mouth.

Carla's voice came out of the inky blackness, "James, It wasn't Alex Kincaid that pushed you down the stairs."

Huh? What was she talking about? Who else could it have been?

"It was Detective Gunne."

Now that just didn't make any sense. Why would Sam have done such a thing? No matter how I tried, I couldn't think of a single logical reason for him to have locked me in here with Carla. He had to know that Alex would be back at some point, that she would find us both now. As far as I could figure out, the only thing he had accomplished was to deliver me into Alex's hands.

"Carla, are you sure? Sam came up here with me searching for you. Why would he do that? Maybe you were dazzled by the sudden light after being here in the dark for a while, maybe your vision was distorted by that. Could that be it?"

"I know what I saw James. He stood there for a few seconds looking down at us so I had a very clear view of him. He looked pissed…really pissed."

I probably would have been staring at her but in the total obscurity of the cellar, all I could do was put my arms around her and try to ease her fear somewhat with my physical presence. At the same time, her words had shaken me to the very core of my soul. If Sam was against us then the situation was really hopeless. We had no way of knowing what was happening above us and that meant no way to plan any kind of escape or reaction should the door above us open up. The one thing I could do that might help was to finish getting Carla loose from all the tape that had been used on her hands and feet. As I worked on the tape, I asked her to fill me in on events from her perspective.

She told me about hearing a noise in the night and getting up to check on it, commenting wryly that she was really glad that she had stopped long enough to use the bathroom before getting dressed to go downstairs. She cried as she told of seeing Flash lying there, obviously dead, on the cold tile floor, blood oozing out around him. She spoke of the attack from behind and her terror as she was forced into the trunk of a car, her assailant still unseen and the pain and fear she had felt while trudging through the forest to this cabin. Then she told me about seeing the look of unholy triumph on Alex Kincaid's face as she fell backwards into the root cellar.

"It was the most gleeful expression I've ever seen outside of a few movies. She was enjoying my pain and the sense of victory over whatever was driving her actions."

By the time she had finished recounting her story, I had finished freeing her from the tape. I shifted around so that I could lean against the wall of the cellar and pulled her over to sit on my lap, so I could wrap my arms around her. I think both of us felt a little better for the physical contact. It gave a sense of orientation in the total darkness which had enveloped us. It made it feel a bit less like we were already disembodied spirits, haunting the night. The comfort would have meant a lot more

to me if my mind hadn't kept coming back to the idea that Sam had turned against us and was apparently working with Alex all along. Could anybody have luck that bad? To have both my lawyer and the detective investigating the case turn out to be part of a conspiracy to commit murder and kidnapping made me understand the trials of Job a whole lot better.

I spent a little time bringing Carla up to date on what had happened in the half-day since she had been kidnapped. Since most of it was just Sam and I floundering to identify who had taken her, and she already knew the answer to that question, it didn't take all that long to get caught up. After that, we just sat there in the dark, holding on to each other for a while. It seemed like we had been down there for hours but it probably wasn't very long at all. It finally dawned on me to use the little face light on my watch to check the time and perhaps give us a few seconds of dim light every once in a while. I held my hand up near our faces and fumbled for a moment before finding the right button. I didn't even see my watch the first time; I was so busy looking at Carla. I eventually determined that we had been together down there for only about fifteen minutes.

I tried lifting the trap door but Sam had apparently put a heavy piece of furniture or something on top of it. It wouldn't budge.

After getting knocked out I wasn't in much better shape than she was, but at least I had shoes on. We had known that she was barefoot when we left town to head up here, but not much else. At least she had been wearing a sweat suit so she hadn't suffered too badly from the cool of the root cellar. Her feet were another story. They were bloody, bruised, and really cold. I couldn't give her shoes to wear but I did give her the thick athletic socks I was wearing and put my shoes back on my bare feet. Neither of us was going to be able to run a marathon this way, but it was something. At least it gave her a little protection and helped warm up her feet which made me feel like I had been able to improve things a tiny bit.

We just sat huddled together in the darkness for a bit while Carla finished recovering from having been horizontal all day. When I first got her loose and she sat upright, the sudden change in position had made her really dizzy and nauseous; a situation that was only made worse by the darkness since it took away any point of reference to help her get her balance back. After a few more minutes, she felt ready to try standing up and I helped her to her feet, holding on to her when she started to sway. She could barely hobble but we needed to get her steady enough that there was a chance of escape if an opportunity came up.

It wasn't long before we heard the sound of somebody moving around in the living area above us. The muffled noise of footsteps across the floor and an unintelligible mumble of somebody speaking. For a moment, we both wondered if we should shout out in case it was the other officers but decided against it. If it was Alex, I didn't want her to know that there was an extra person in the cellar and that Carla was free from her bonds. If it was Sam, well he already knew where we were. It might be the cops, but if Sam was really the enemy, then he probably hadn't called for backup at all.

In the end, we scrunched up against the wall as best we could in hopes of being out of sight if the trap door were opened. For both Alex and Sam that would give us a split second of surprise when they looked down into an apparently empty space, if it was the backup officers then we would just announce our presence and step into view. In whispered tones, we discussed a plan of action, Carla suggesting that the best plan would be for her to be in plain view while I hid in the shadows. That way, I could either surprise whoever it was when they came down to get her (assuming they did) or follow quietly until

I could get the jump on them if they just made her go up. I can't say that I liked the idea of using her as bait while I cowered in the shadows, but her plan did make sense and ultimately, I agreed.

There was a scraping noise overhead and then the trap door was raised and a beam of bright light blazed down, momentarily blinding us as our eyes struggled to adjust. From my dark corner, I could see Alex standing in the opening. She was holding a gun in her right hand and it was pointed at Carla's head.

"Carla? I see you have managed to get out of all that tape I used. You're a resourceful woman, Bravo. Good news for me to since it makes my task so much simpler. I had been considering how to release your feet so you could walk without getting kicked for my trouble. I was afraid I was going to have to knock you out again first and that would have wasted a lot of time that I just don't have any more. Now, be a good girl and come up here." She waved the gun a bit to emphasize her point.

Unfortunately, as Carla slowly limped to the steps, Alex noticed the damn socks that I had given her.

"Now where on Earth did you get that pair of socks from? I know that root cellar was completely empty and they are way too big for you anyway. Is there somebody down there with you?"

As she spoke, she stepped to the side and peered down into my corner. I couldn't rush her because Carla was now blocking the steps.

"I know you must be down there. Come out on your own or I will close this door and just set fire to the building. When they find your body in the burnt out building, they won't have any evidence left to know what happened. I really would rather not do it that way, I rather like this cabin and would like to keep using it, but I will if you force me to it."

Apparently, Sam hadn't told her that I was here

because she looked utterly shocked to find me standing in the gloom.

"Just how did you end up down there James?"

She shook her head in dismay at my apparent ineptness at getting trapped with her victim.

"Why don't you come up here and join us?"

As I headed up behind Carla, the monologue from Alex continued, "I have to say James, I'm a bit disappointed in you. As knights in shining armor go, you seem to be a bit lacking. I assume that you came out here to rescue Carla, but to let yourself get captured instead just doesn't seem to inspire much confidence. What about you Carla, does his role

of gallant knight instill you with confidence? Make you feel all warm and safe? It probably would have been much more effective if he had actually managed to rescue you, don't you think? Still, he did manage to find you at least, that has to count for something I suppose."

By that point, I had reached the top and stood next to Carla. The gun in Alex's hand pointed between us in a way that made me believe that she could, and would, shoot either one in a split second if we moved wrong. Her conversational tone was also beginning to get on my nerves. The way she was chit chatting as if this were a normal and non-lethal situation was incredibly obnoxious. Even worse was the fact that she could manage such normalcy in this bizarre scenario; it just seemed to be further proof of how completely crazy she was. I didn't dare try to make a move yet. As long as she was keeping us alive for some reason, I could wait for the right moment to make my move. There was no sign of Sam and I decided that if she didn't know he was around, I wasn't going to tell her. Whether he was on our side or not, if he appeared unexpectedly at some point, it might give me enough of the element of surprise to be the difference between life and death. For now, we would play along. Besides, I was kind of hoping that maybe someplace along the way she could be induced to explain things to us. If I had to die, I at least would like to know why.

EIGHTEEN

Nothing had ever felt as good as seeing James' face appear above me when that trapdoor opened. It had been such an incredible relief to see a friendly face. The relief turned to ashes when I saw detective Gunne shove James forward into the open air. I will never forget the look on Sam's face, framed by the square of light formed by the opening. He looked furious. He didn't say a word, just motioned for me to be silent, and then dropped the lid back down plunging me back into darkness. If I survived this, I would probably have to sleep with a light on forever. There was a sound like something heavy being slid across the floor above us and then receding footsteps. I figured that he must have pushed the sofa or some other large piece of furniture onto the trap door, making it a trap for real. I was totally at a loss, why would Sam have done such a thing. When I saw James I had thought I was rescued, then this. Obviously, Sam and James had come here together, so why would Sam trap his partner down here with me? The only thing I could think of was that Sam had been in this with Alex all along. It didn't matter much that I had no clue why he might be helping her since I had no idea why she was doing any of these things either.

I gave up for the moment on trying to understand what was going on and concentrated on listening to see if James was still breathing. He had fallen near me, but tied up the way I was, I couldn't reach him, I couldn't even ask if he was OK. I squirmed around like a worm on a hook until my ear was near his head, a point I found by running into it with my own aching skull, and tried to listen for breath sounds. I thought I heard them, but in the darkness, I had heard so many odd things that I couldn't be sure. In the end I just had to wait for him to wake up on his own, which he did after a little bit.

Once he woke up, he reached out and found me in the darkness pretty quickly. When he did, he started to work at getting the tape off my mouth. The whole time he was working on that, he kept telling me that everything would be OK that Sam had gone to call for backup and we would be free soon. I kept trying to shake my head at that, but it just hampered his efforts to uncover my mouth so I finally just held still until he was done. Damn but it hurt to have that tape pulled off of my face. As soon as it was gone, I told him that Sam was the one who had pushed him into the cellar. I don't think he believed me at first but eventually I convinced him that I really had seen Sam push him. He was quiet for a couple minutes after that, I think it took a while for him to absorb the fact that the person who was supposed to be the good guy in all this, probably wasn't. I'm not sure but he might even have been feeling a bit guilty for having led Sam here. All along though, he kept working on getting the rest of that noxious tape off me so that I could finally move. I had been lying on that dirt floor all day long and everything hurt, especially my feet which were freezing. The only good thing about that was that they were practically numb and therefore they didn't hurt quite as bad as they had when I first got there. Once I was completely free we moved over to the wall and just sat together for a little bit. It felt so nice to just sit there and be held. It was almost enough to make me forget the circumstances, almost but not quite.

So much horrible stuff had happened in the past week that I just wanted to curl up and give in to it all. Gus and Flash had been murdered and I had been kidnapped. Now my would-be rescuer was trapped with me and the only other people who knew where we were...were the bad guys. A good crying jag would have been appropriate about then, but I couldn't afford to waste the time on it. I had been thinking all day about what, if anything, I could do to save myself if a chance came up. I had been lying there in the dark pretty much reviewing everything I had ever seen or heard in the news or in movies, about people that did (and didn't) survive kidnappings, trying to create contingency plans that probably would never be of any use in reality. You have to do something to keep your sanity, trapped in the dark. What I did was plot escapes.

Eventually James and I got down to the business of figuring out what to do when Alex (or Sam) came back. I felt that we had no choice; we had to assume the worst for planning purposes, the worst being that Sam and Alex were in it together, that Sam had told Alex we were both down here and that they were smart enough to know that James would have gotten me free of the tape bindings. He didn't like it much but I convinced him that we had to play it safe, put me back out where I was visible and have him hide in case a chance to surprise somebody popped up. I didn't think it was likely, but it made sense to at least prepare for the chance.

Unfortunately, Alex was smarter than we realized and when she grasped that I wasn't taped up anymore, she made me come up the steps instead of coming down to get me. When she looked around and saw James, he couldn't get the jump on her because I was in his way. In the end, we both found ourselves standing in the living room staring down the barrel of her gun. We stood there staring mutely at her while she chattered inanely at us. How she could act like she had just met two old friends on the street while holding us at gunpoint was completely beyond comprehension. Her matter-of-fact manner was horribly chilling. Eventually, she wound down and paused to look at James.

"You should have just let things be James. I really liked you, but you had to go and follow me up here. You could have had it all. Your freedom and me as well but you just couldn't let go of your "old" friend Carla, could you? You had to go sticking your nose in my business."

The gun wavered back and forth between us as she spoke.

"You realize of course that I can't afford to let you live, don't you? It's a real shame to. I haven't had that much fun in bed in years. For what it's worth, you really were good."

I knew she was trying to goad me into a reaction and I

have to admit, the mental image of them in bed together bothered me, more than I would have expected, but I wasn't about to give her the satisfaction.

"Alex, if you're trying to get a reaction out of me, don't bother. James and I were over long ago, nothing left but some fond memories. If he had a good time in your bed, then I'm glad he enjoyed it. Although how he could bring himself to sleep with a psychopathic bitch of your caliber escapes me at the moment."

I looked up at him and winked with the eye facing away from her,

"I'm a bit surprised though, you usually have better taste. I suppose...every man needs to drop his standards occasionally though, just for the fun of it."

For a split second, she looked like she was going to pull the trigger, which wasn't exactly the effect I was going for. I was hoping to keep her off balance by not only not showing my fear, but throwing things back at her. If I could keep her distracted enough, an opening might occur for James to take action. Obviously she was more eager to do me harm than she was him. It made a weird kind of sense. After all, she did kidnap me and had apparently planned on keeping him around. She recovered instantly though and gave a smile that could have frozen blood before motioning for us to move out the door.

"Enough chit chat let's get moving. I have plans for tomorrow and really don't want to miss them. Out the door and up the path to the left, both of you."

As we turned and headed out across the front porch and down the steps to the path, James took my arm to help support me as I struggled to hobble along.

"How sweet, still taking care of others James? Always trying to save every stray in sight."

For some reason her words sounded very familiar. I

couldn't quite remember when or where but I knew that I had heard somebody else say that, in just the same tone of voice. I shook my head as if that would help shake out the obstacle that was keeping me from remembering but it didn't help.

I gave James a puzzled look and saw the same question in his eyes. Both of us apparently had a sense of déjà vu that was totally out of sync with the situation and making everything feel that much creepier. James went for a different tactic than I had, trying to get Alex to explain her reasons for everything she had done. Either she really did like him or she figured it didn't matter what we knew before we died. As we staggered along through the woods, she began to talk more and more about everything.

"Why did I kill Gus? You really want to know why? That man destroyed my mother and ruined my life. My whole horrible childhood was his fault. My mother virtually killed herself with drugs and alcohol because of him. I blame him for it all; every rotten, revolting thing my mother's "boyfriends" did to me as a child and adolescent. Did you know some of them only slept with her so they could get access to her pretty little daughter? She knew. It didn't matter to her. He did that to her...and to me. I searched for years for that man and when I finally found him, I made sure that he would never hurt me or anyone else again. I sure did. I found out where he was 5 years ago, but I took my time. I planned it all out so perfectly. I bought the cabin and the house in his name, did you know that? I had to wait for the right place to become available, an estate auction for a deceased owner with no heirs was perfect. Then I had other lawyers handle the transactions for me so that there was no paper trail that could be traced to me. I thought it was funny that he owned the house I was living in and didn't even know it. He owed me that much anyway. That and a whole lot more, but most of it could never be made right, so all I could do was make sure that I stopped him from doing the same to anybody else."

James and I had stopped dead in our tracks and turned to

look at her in amazement. The incredible bile spilling from her was like nothing either of us had ever seen before. She was raving, but the gun never moved in her hand. She waved the gun again and motioned off the trail and deeper into the woods. Before we set off again, James asked her exactly what Gus had done to ruin her life. She wasn't buying it as a reason to delay but once we started walking again, she resumed her diatribe.

"He ruined my mother's life, I told you that. He ruined her and in return, she tried to destroy me. She tried really hard, but I'm so much stronger than that. I wouldn't let her break me. The last time she tried, I finally got the chance to stop her forever. Do you know that they rarely do an autopsy on known drug addicts? At least not when they are found with a syringe in their arm and extremely pure heroin in their veins. She had been in and out of rehab so many times, had fallen off the wagon over and over; nobody was surprised when she turned up dead. Nobody even questioned how a woman with no money at all, who was selling both herself and her 14 year old daughter for a fix, managed to get her hands on stuff that high grade."

James tried again, "Alex, exactly how did he ruin her life? What did he DO to her?"

Her laughter echoed through the woods around us, "James, James, James, you just don't get it do you? Gus was my father."

Into the stunned silence she announced, "Here we are."

Almost before her bomb about Gus had reached my brain, we were staring into an open gravesite.

"I had planned on killing Carla and burying her here. I can shovel dirt on two just as easily as one though so this will work out just fine."

I was still stuck on Gus being her father. "Alex, I don't understand; if Gus was your father, why did you kill him? I would have thought you would be happy to finally have found him."

"Oh yeah, I was happy alright. Happy that all my searching had finally paid off, happy that I was finally going to have some peace once I knew that both of them were gone. He refused to marry my mother when she got pregnant, claimed that the baby wasn't his. She was only a teenager for goodness sake, what was she supposed to do in this dinky little town with a baby and no husband? Her parents threw her out, sent her to a home for unwed mothers in Kansas City so that nobody in town would know their shame at having a pregnant teenage daughter. I would have destroyed them as well but God had already taken care of them for me by the time I found them. I had to settle for taking care of Gus by himself. I moved to town and made friends with him and his little wife. Took care of your doggie for you, so that I could make a copy of the house key. Spent most of the time I was dog sitting digging through everything in the house to find the right way to kill him without getting caught. Once I knew where the insulin was kept, it was a pretty simple thing to use the key and sneak back in at a future date to ruin it. I waited until enough time had passed to be sure that I wouldn't be a suspect and took care of it. Since there was no way to be sure what order the bottles would be used in, it provided that much more uncertainty for the cops when they tried to figure it out. Of course that was assuming they figured out that he was murdered and didn't just take for granted that as a diabetic, he must have eaten something he shouldn't have. It figures that being a prominent citizen like he was, they would actually do an autopsy to be sure of the cause of death. Satisfied now? You know why I killed him so this little tête-à-tête is over. Get over next to the edge of the hole, both of you."

I saw a movement behind her and realized that it was Sam Gunne, working his way slowly closer. He was obviously trying to be quiet and had just as obviously been hurt, there was blood running down his face and into his eyes. He was holding one hand to his head in a way that made me think that somebody had hit him pretty hard. He held a finger up to his lips for quiet and continued to creep up on Alex. I realized that I had to keep her talking just a little bit longer if we were going to survive this.

"I can see why you killed Gus, but why did you kidnap me and bring me out here if you were going to kill me anyway? "

"Oh come on Carla, you can figure it out if you really want to. There was nothing to link me to Gus' murder. Once he was dead I should have finally been at peace, but then I realized that it was partly your fault as well. He married you; he must have chosen you over my mother. If you hadn't lured him away from her, my life might have been very different. Not only that, but you were a temptation to James as well. I realized that when he kept talking about you, worried that you might actually believe that he had something to do with your poor husband's demise. I saw the way you clung to him at the funeral. It wasn't his fault. He didn't know what kind of a Jezebel you were. Luring men away from the women they were meant to be with. You stole my father; I wasn't going to let you steal James as well. I just didn't count on him getting all gallant and figuring out what I had done. I knew he wouldn't understand why I was doing it; men just don't really understand these things. You do though, don't you? I got rid of that damned dog while I was at it, just because Gus had loved it so much."

I'm pretty sure that James had seen the detective as well that point, because he chimed in with a question of his own. "Did you really think you would get away with kidnapping Carla?"

"Actually, I did. I was reasonably certain that I didn't leave any fingerprints and such, and there were no motives that anybody could possible know of to link me to Carla. Which reminds me, just how did you and detective Gunne managed to track me down. Yes, I know he came up here with you, but I took care of him already. He's back near the house, unconscious. I'll just have to bury him there because I can't carry him this far."

"Is that why you kept Carla alive all this time? Because you couldn't carry her?'

She gave him a grin, "Of course it was. I'm not exactly stupid you know. I knew that there was no way I could possibly move her body and getting rid of it altogether was really the only option. I kept her alive and made her walk all the way to her own graveside. Macabre, isn't it? So, how did you figure out that it was me?"

Sam was only about 5 feet away now so James only needed to keep her talking for a few more seconds.

"You left a couple of long blond hairs on the side gate when you took Carla. Your hairdresser Lorraine figured it out and told us who the hair probably belonged to."

Sam's voice came from right behind her causing her to whip around and moving the gun's aim away from us. The instant that happened; James launched himself at her; hitting her in the small of the back just as Sam's fist connected with her jaw. I watched from the graveside as she collapsed on top of James, her body limp and her arms tangled around him in a ghastly parody of an embrace. Sam picked up her gun from where it had fallen, mere inches from her outstretched hand, and tucked it into his waistband. Once that was done, he leaned over and helped James extricate himself from her and stand up, then turned and called the rest of the cops who appeared to have been lagging behind in reaching us.

James was glaring at Sam and finally just let loose and slugged him, catching him on the jaw. His head snapped back so hard that it was almost surprising that his neck wasn't broken and even more of a surprise when he just calmly reached up and rubbed his jaw, smiling at James.

"You bastard, you set us up, didn't you? You shoved me down that cellar knowing that she would come back for

Carla. Couldn't you at least have warned us of what you were up to? You damn near scared us both to death, thinking that you had changed sides."

I watched in amazement as he railed at Sam. This was a side of James that I had never seen before. He was usually the peacemaker. Thinking back, I can't remember ever seeing him raise a hand against anyone in all the years that I had known him. Sam just stood there and took it, probably because he knew that James was right; it had been a rotten thing for him to do to us.

Eventually, James wound down and Sam managed to get his side in. "Actually, using you as bait wasn't exactly what I had in mind. I just couldn't think of any other way to get you to stay put. I told you to stay outside in the shadows while I called for backup, but just like back in town, you ignored me and went barreling into a building when we had no idea what might be there and with no backup in place. I knew that you would get Mrs. Barnes untied while I hunted for Alex. Unfortunately, she found me first and hit me over the head, knocked me out like a light. She left me out cold behind the cabin while she went to take care of her hostage. Fortunately, you all were moving pretty slowly and all of that conversation made you easy to locate. By the time I came to, you must have been halfway here. I met up with the guys and we got here just in time to hear the end of her story."

"You could have warned us."

"There wasn't time. When I pushed you, I could already hear movement in the woods nearby. I needed to find cover pretty fast if I was going to have any chance of surprising her. Unfortunately, I wasn't fast enough and she caught me by surprise."

All of us were so intent on our conversation that we really weren't paying much attention to Alex. That turned out to be a mistake. As James turned back towards me and Sam shifted to call out to the other officers, she erupted from the ground like a volcano. Her face a mask of insane fury, she grabbed for the gun in his waistband. In the struggle, she managed to get the gun free and fired off a wild shot at Sam before two of the other officers shot her. The bullet from her gun passed through Sam's upper arm causing a nasty but non-lethal wound. The bullets from the two officers had been considerably more precise.

EPILOGUE

"You know what they say about bleached blondes, don't you? Only their hairdresser knows for sure."

We all groaned at him but Sam was

unrepentant, claiming that it was a perfectly appropriate quotation for describing how the case was finally solved.

We had gathered at Carla's since she still wasn't getting out much while her feet healed. It was also a good idea to stay close to the house to watch out for the kitten I had gotten for her. Somehow, I didn't think another dog would work out too well under the circumstances but wanted her to have some companionship available any time she needed it.

Since it was too soon after Gus' death for me to be providing that kind of 24/7 presence, I had driven almost 200 miles to pick up an eight week old Chocolate Siamese kitten for her. It was rather adorable and a stroke of near genius on my part. His name was Charlie and his clumsy antics and playful nature made him an excellent balm for her emotional wounds.

Sam had arrived just minutes earlier and to our surprise, he had Suzanne with him. That relationship seemed to be progressing well.

Ever since he had gotten himself shot in the arm while struggling with Alex, Suzanne had been dotting over him like a mother hen with only one chick. To watch them together, you would think that they had been together for years.

The four of us were enjoying a sumptuous meal of pizza and beer while Sam caught us up to date on things from the investigation of Alex's background. Her name was actually Alexis Moorehouse and she had never been in foster care. Her mother was alive and well. In fact, she was a middle class housewife in Boca Raton, Florida.

Alex had been in and out of mental institutions a good part of her life, suffering from delusions that had begun after a high fever when she was in the 4th grade. She had never been to college and had never taken the bar.

When it came right down to it, everything that had happened was a result of her delusions. None of it had been real, except the part about Gus being her father. DNA tests had shown that he really was and her mother had confirmed it; although her husband had adopted Alexis as a baby.

It turned out that her mother had come from right here in Element and had been a classmate of Gus' in high school. She really had gotten pregnant and left town but she had never told Gus that he was a father.

The conversation continued as the food supply dwindled. Suzanne began regaling Carla with the story of how us poor mindless men had been getting ready to go all over town playing the Princes Not-So-Charming in search an Anti- Cinderella. Her animated storytelling eventually reduced all of us to hysterical laughter.

The kitten had been wildly attacking the tiny bright red dot of light from a laser pointer as we made it whirl madly about the room. His fur bristled as he leapt and pounced on the bright, elusive spot. Eventually, fatigue overcame ferocity and his energy gave out. He made circles in my lap, tiny claws pricking my leg, then curled up in a tiny ball sleeping the sound sleep of the very young and innocent.

It seemed like a good sign.

ABOUT THE AUTHOR

MJ Buck is a U.S Navy veteran with a Bachelor's degree from the State University of New York Empire State College. Her many years of experience as a firefighter's wife and a supporting volunteer in rural fire departments have shaped her exceptional insight into this high adrenaline world. She currently lives in Maryland where, with the help of her firefighter husband and two discriminating feline editors, she is working on her next novel.